Messing *with the* Billionaire

MAID IN MIAMI BOOK 1

BREEZIE BENNETT

THE MAID IN MIAMI SERIES

Messing With The Billionaire
Messing With The Bad Boy
Messing With The Bartender
Messing With The Bodyguard
Messing With The Ballplayer

For a complete list, buy links, and reading order of all my books, visit www.breeziebennett.com. Be sure to sign up for my newsletter to find out when the next book is released!

PROLOGUE

LILLY
May 7, 2019 — University of Florida Business School Graduation Day

"We did it, girls." I plop down on the world's most well-loved sectional in the living room of our apartment, dramatically tossing my graduation cap into the air.

"Heck yeah, we did." Bianca Lopez, the fun and wild member of our little five-person girl gang, pops open a bottle of champagne, waving it around as it fizzes. "Let's get lit! Who wants to go out? Hit the town?"

"No, thank you." Meredith Fleming holds up a hand and shakes her head.

"Miss Goodie Two-Shoes, don't you ever want to be a *little* bit spontaneous?" Bianca urges Meredith, our favorite perfectionist who's never met a rule or regulation she didn't follow.

Meredith rolls her big, hazel-colored eyes and curls up on the couch next to me. "My mom is coming over early in the morning to help me move all of my stuff out, so I can't—"

"Stop." I hold up a hand and squeeze my eyes shut dramatically. "Don't even talk about moving out. Those words are banned for the night. I am *so* not ready to accept the fact that the five of us will never live together again. I don't want school to be over," I whine, grabbing a pink and blue floral throw pillow and hugging it to my chest.

"I feel you." Aubrey Shepard walks over to the living room, dropping her graduation cap down onto the coffee table and kicking off her heels. "How is it possible that all five of us just graduated from one of the best public business schools in the country and *none* of us have a job lined up?"

"It's a dog-eat-dog world out there," Bianca says on a sigh, pouring the bubbly champagne into a few of our plastic flutes. She waves a glass in front of Meredith. "Come on, Four Point O. That GPA alone deserves to be celebrated."

Meredith takes the glass and laughs dryly. "Not like that perfect GPA has gotten me anything. My future is every bit as uncertain as all of yours."

"For the love of all that is holy, get these things off my feet." Cici Chen, who was trailing behind as we walked into the apartment, rips off her four-inch wedges and resentfully throws them onto the ground.

"Hi, Ci." I pat the open spot on the couch next to me. "Come sit."

"My toes may never recover," she groans, absent-mindedly taking a glass of champagne that Bianca passes to her.

Aubrey giggles. "You wore heels for, like, two hours."

"Two miserable, grueling, agonizing hours." Cici flips her long, shiny black hair over her shoulders as she sits down. "You guys were totally wrong. I absolutely could have walked across the stage in my Nikes."

We all laugh and settle into the living room—the cozy, homey space with tapestries decorating the walls and plants in every corner. Mismatched throw pillows and blankets clutter the couch; no matter how many times a day Meredith fixes them, they always end up in messy piles.

The apartment that's held way too many late-night study sessions and *Bachelor* viewing parties...the place that's held a thousand tears and a million laughs and has been our home for all of business school...will be vacant in a couple days.

I glance around at my four best friends in the entire world. The five of us arguably some of the most unlikely friends in the world who bonded over business school and came to absolutely adore each other's differences.

There's Bianca, the bubbly party girl who pushes everyone out of their shells and has given us thousands of amazing and hilarious memories. Aubrey, the cautious, logical thinker who aced every accounting class that was thrown at her and has never taken a risk in her life. She keeps us all in check. Sweet Meredith, the kind, gentle perfect one whose innocent heart is so golden that it's actually impossible to be jealous of her amazing grades and stellar test scores. And Cici, our beloved tomboy, who yells at the TV during football Sundays and makes us all go to the gym with her, even when we really don't feel like it.

And then...there's me. Lilly McCarthy, MBA. *Apparently.*

My friends would probably call me the optimist, the dreamer, the one who never runs out of hope, even when Aubrey attempts to bring me back down to earth.

But right now...hope seems a little bit scarce. What's a degree worth if you don't have any plans to actually use it?

A chilling and unfamiliar melancholy feeling ripples through me, the cool nostalgia that accompanies the end of an era. A wonderful, fun-filled, happy and energizing era.

And the next era? I have no idea what it holds. I know opportunity will come, I know I'll make it for myself, but the not knowing is unsettling.

I decide to shake off the heavy future questions and just enjoy what is likely to be the very last night all five of us are in *our* apartment together.

It's all going to be okay. I know it is. I just have to figure it out.

"Knock it down, Georgia Brown." Bianca tips the bottom of Meredith's champagne glass, making her finish the rest of it in one big gulp.

"Let's go Mer, let's go!" Cici chants, as if she's cheering on the Miami Heat in the NBA finals.

Meredith lowers her glass and makes a face, laughing as she shakes her head.

"Pass that bottle my way." I wave a hand at Bianca, gesturing for the champagne.

"Don't worry." She gives a smile, pushing back a strand of her long, brown hair. "There's a lot more where that came from."

As the champagne flows and the night goes from late to later, we sit and talk and laugh and reminisce, all stuck in the confusing and exciting mess of being twenty-three and having no plans.

At one point Bianca starts blasting our throwback hits playlist over the speaker, and somehow we all end up dancing around the living room and the kitchen.

We all cackle with laughter as Aubrey drops it low and Meredith attempts to twerk, stumbling and falling onto her butt with a bout of giggles.

"Mer's drunk!" I exclaim, feeling my own waves of warmth from the bubbly bottles we've now knocked down quite a few of.

"I am not," Meredith insists, although the pink flush in her cheeks and her silly smile says otherwise, as she places her hands on my shoulders and laughs.

"You guys!" Cici holds her arms out wide, bringing all of us in for a close group hug. "Last night in apartment two oh six."

"Stop saying that," I whine, laughing softly into the close embrace of my best friends. "I seriously can't handle it."

"I'm so surprised, Lilly," Aubrey says as we pull away, searching my face. "I would have thought you'd be all jazzed about the future. On to the next thing, right?" Her brown eyes are wide with understanding and kindness.

I let out a breath. "I want to be excited, but the truth is...I'm kinda scared."

Bianca lowers the volume of the music as we all sit back down on the couch and lay on the floor, splayed over the mountains of colorful blankets and pillows.

"You and me both," Aubrey admits, tucking her knees into her chest. "According to a recent study I read, business school graduates currently have the lowest rate of employment in the last fifty years."

"Thanks for that, Captain Sunshine." Bianca chuckles and takes a swig of a bottle, ignoring the plastic champagne flutes that we seemingly abandoned a while ago.

"What time is it?" Meredith asks, lying flat on her back and staring at the ceiling. "My mom is gonna be here at seven-thirty."

Bianca cackles. "It's almost five."

Meredith shoots up, her light brown hair falling in soft waves around her delicate, pale, beautiful face. "In the morning?!"

Cici laughs and puffs out a sigh. "The whole night has passed, and we still haven't figured out our futures."

Aubrey shakes her head. "Not even one of us."

"Hey." Bianca lifts an almost empty bottle of champagne. "A toast. To the five of us. We may be jobless, but what we lack in income, we make up for in fabulosity."

We all pick up a bottle or a glass—some empty, some full—and lift them up, forming a circle on the living room floor.

"To the best friends I've ever had," Meredith says.

"To lifelong friendship," Aubrey adds.

Cici smiles and clinks the top of a bottle. "Wherever life takes us, we'll always have each other's backs."

"Forever," I chime in, swallowing the lump of emotion that rises in my throat. I love these girls with everything I have, and that seems to be the only thing that's certain right now.

We all drink to our emotional and tipsy toasts, hugging

more and laughing through the occasional bout of bitter-sweet tears.

"Wait!" Meredith jumps up, suddenly excited about something. "You said it's past five AM, right?"

"Yeah..." Aubrey cocks her head and we all turn to look at Mer.

"That means final thesis grades are posted!" She starts frantically thumbing on her iPhone.

"Mer..." Bianca rolls her eyes. "We all just *graduated*. I think we know we passed."

"But I would like to know my exact final grade." Meredith sticks her tongue out and straightens her shoulders.

"I kinda wanna know, too." I reach in my pocket and pull out my phone to open up the transcript. "I put an insane amount of work into that project."

I think back on my final thesis project for business school. We were required to put together a thorough, top-to-bottom business plan for an original company. It had to include every last detail of the business, right down to expense sheets and budgets and hiring plans. The idea was that the proposal is so accurate and well-thought-out, it could theoretically be an actual start-up if someone followed the project to a T.

"Y'all are loco." Bianca twirls her hair. "This place is just lucky I even *finished* that project."

"Didn't you turn it in late?" Aubrey asks her with a soft laugh.

"Only like a day." Bianca lifts a shoulder.

"Classic B." Cici rolls her eyes and also reaches in her pocket to see the final grade. "Come on, let's all check."

"Ninety-four," Meredith says suddenly, breathing a sigh of relief. "I'll take it."

"Eighty-nine!" Cici exclaims. "Wow, professor must have liked my idea for a women-only gym."

"I want that to exist," I say, waiting as my page takes forever to load. "I genuinely want that to exist."

"Woohoo!" Bianca fist bumps. "Eighty-one! I'm above average, ladies."

Meredith gives her a sweet smile. "B, not one single thing about you is average."

"Come here, chica." She squeezes Mer's slender shoulders in a tight hug.

"Ninety for me." Aubrey shrugs. "Thank God."

"As if there was ever any doubt." Cici ruffles her hair.

Suddenly, all four sets of beautiful, sleepy, and slightly intoxicated eyes are on me.

"What about you, Lil?" Bianca urges. "You had a cool idea for that project, as I recall."

"Oh, yeah!" Meredith sits up enthusiastically. "You created that whole high-end cleaning company. The one that caters to millionaires and celebrities and fancy people."

"That was mine, yeah." I smile, glancing down at the freaking page on my phone that still isn't loading.

Is the Wi-Fi out or something?

"I did really like that one." Aubrey points at me, sipping champagne. "The need for a company like that actually makes a lot of sense, and the margin of profit would be massive considering the client base."

"Not to mention..." Bianca shimmies her shoulders. "Hello, hot rich guys, anyone? What a fun job. You know, if it was real and not just a figment of our dear Lilly's imagination."

Meredith shoves her and rolls her eyes. "You definitely had the best idea of the bunch, Lilly."

"We'll see if Dr. Harrison agreed." I swallow nervously as I attempt to refresh my student login page.

A couple beats pass as the page reloads, and the grade for my final project of business school pops up on the screen.

100.

"What?" I blurt out in complete disbelief, laughing in shock as I stare at the number on my phone.

"What is it?" Meredith asks eagerly.

"Yeah, Lil. Tell us!" Cici insists.

"I..." I choke on the words, bringing my hand to my mouth as I process the victory. "I got a hundred," I say softly.

"You *what*?" Bianca shrieks.

"Lilly!" Meredith squeals, rushing across the carpet to hug me. "That's amazing!"

"Holy heck, girl." Aubrey shakes her head in disbelief. "Harrison doesn't give perfect scores. Ever. It's statistically unreal."

"That's our Lilly!" Cici raises another glass. "To a perfect score!"

Happiness washes over me as we toast again and laugh as the sun starts to come up, peeking through the pink and yellow curtains of the living room with its soft, early light.

We all sit around, each of us still wearing our graduation dresses, exhausted and confused and overwhelmed.

But my mind keeps going back to that project. A hundred percent? Aubrey is right, it really is unheard of.

The project was good. Really freaking good. And before I have a chance to think or consider or hesitate, a wild idea comes flying out of my very optimistic mouth, hushing the hum of conversation. "We should do it."

The groups falls silent at this, all of them looking at me confused.

"Do what?" Aubrey asks.

"My project." I nod slowly, standing up off the living room floor as this crazy idea starts to rapidly materialize in my head. "The five of us should start a high-end cleaning business. Exactly the way it's planned out in my proposal."

"Lil…" Aubrey cocks her head, the wheels in her brain already turning with the logistics and practicalities.

Cici chokes on a laugh, her straight, black hair falling all around her face as she stares up at me. "Wait a second. Are you *serious*?"

"I mean…why the heck not?" Excitement zings through me as I pace around the living room, watching each skeptical set of eyes studying me like I'm a crazy person.

"Lilly, your project was amazing." Aubrey stretches her arms over her head. "But, we can't *really* start our own business. I mean the cost of capital alone would be astronomical, not to mention—"

"We could get a loan," Bianca chimes in, meeting my gaze with a glimmer in her eye.

Hope rises in my chest. B is on board.

"Exactly," I agree. "With a proposal this detailed and well-thought-out? We could easily get a loan to start the business up."

"I don't know, Lilly..." Meredith pushes her hair behind her ears, shaking her head. "Starting a company is an enormous undertaking. We'd have to do everything right, make no mistakes."

I gesture at her and smile. "Good thing we have the Queen of Perfection on our team."

"You know..." Cici stands up, slowly nodding as a smile pulls at her soft, delicate cheeks. "This actually could be something. This actually could work."

"I'm totally in." Bianca turns to me, grinning brightly with a charged enthusiasm in her expression. "If not us, then who?"

"A high-end cleaning company..." Aubrey leans against the sofa and lets out a noisy sigh, thinking hard. "We'd have to be located somewhere that would have a high demand for something like that."

I look around at the group of us, remembering the only thing we all five have in common.

We're all from Miami.

"Let's go home," I say, wrapping my arms around Cici and Bianca and squeezing them close. "Let's go home and do it in Miami."

"We are all made in Miami, after all." Meredith lifts a shoulder.

"Made in Miami..." I repeat under my breath, turning to Bianca. "*Maid* In Miami. That's the name of the business!"

"Holy genius!" Bianca jumps up and high fives me with both hands.

"I'm on board." Cici flips her hair. "I bet if we really got this thing going, we could attract the professional sports industry. They've got huge complexes and training facilities and constantly need professional cleaning services."

"Amazing!" I exclaim. "We'll hire a staff. And the five of us will oversee everything, with one of us going on-site to every project."

"It'll be done *right*," Meredith adds, standing up to join Cici, Aubrey, and me at the front of the living room. "With the highest level of professionalism, quality, and class. I'll make sure of it."

"And fun! It'll be all about fun, too," Bianca chimes in.

"And friendship," I say, smiling so hard my cheeks hurt.

"That leaves you, Aub." Bianca juts her chin to Aubrey, who is still sitting on the couch staring at the four of us, her face riddled with concern and hesitation.

"I don't know, you guys. It's kind of a crazy idea. I mean there are just so many things we'd have to figure out and plan for and...this is a massive, serious, insanely huge undertaking."

"And that's why we need you," I insist, walking over to the couch and reaching both my hands out to take hers. "You keep us grounded. You'd handle all the logic and numbers and analysis and make sure everything makes sense."

Aubrey shrugs, a reluctant smile tugging at her lips. "I am good at that."

"The very best." I squeeze her hands and pull her up off the couch. "Please, Aub?"

"Come on, Aubrey," Bianca sings. "You know you want to."

"Aubrey! Aubrey! Aubrey!" Cici and Meredith chant through laughter.

"All right, all right." Aubrey waves her hand, shaking her head as if she can't believe what she's about to say. "Let's start a business."

"Woohoo!"

We laugh and cheer and make one last champagne toast as the sun rises over Gainesville, bathing us in a warm glow of happiness and relief.

Because now...we don't have to say goodbye to each other. All we have to do is say hello to our brand-new future. And man, is it bright.

ONE

LILLY
Two Years Later

"Latte for you, Miss Mer?" I breeze into the Maid In Miami headquarters office, which is nestled in a small corner of a tall office building on Brickell.

We're still working out of the same office space we rented when we first started the company, but with all five of us and our growing business, the space is becoming cramped and tight.

"We need a bigger office," I remark, looking around at all of our desks backed up basically against one another throughout the little room.

Thankfully, big windows allow sunshine to pour in, which makes it feel bright and airy, despite the close quarters.

Meredith squints at her computer screen, lowering her glasses. "Absolutely." She reaches out and takes the cup from me. "And I second the office thing. Is it in the budget yet, Aubs?"

"And one for you. And you." I float through the office, handing a coffee to Aubrey and then one to Cici, who are both locked in on their phones or computers.

"Thank you, my darling." Cici blows me a kiss, keeping her eyes glued to the screen in front of her.

Aubrey taps on her keyboard and puffs out a breath. "With current Miami real estate prices, we'll be lucky if we can get ten more square feet with our budget for that."

"Great." Cici sips her coffee. "Big office will have to wait."

"Lilly!" Meredith pops up out of her desk chair, rushing over to me. "It's almost nine-thirty. You're sched-uled to do a consultation with a new prospective client at ten. Shouldn't you be going?"

"At ease, Mer." I smile and take a deep breath. "I'm leaving in a minute."

"Good, because we need an A-1 first impression," Aubrey chimes in, getting up from her desk on the other side of the office to walk over to us. "This guy is a big deal."

"All our clients are big deals," Cici chimes in.

"Yeah, but this guy is different." Aubrey narrows her gaze, her green eyes flashing. "He's a billionaire. With a B."

I blink back in surprise, pulling out my phone to glance at the notes on my schedule. "Really? I totally forgot that. I have his name down as...Theodore Rinehart," I read off the phone screen and wrinkle my nose. "He sounds old."

"Old and loaded." Aubrey holds up a finger. "Theodore Rinehart, hedge fund manager and billionaire."

"Huh. Wow. This one really *is* a big deal." I sip my

latte, nerves and excitement jolting through me as the caffeine settles in.

"Which is why"—Meredith raises her brows—"you don't want to be late."

"Speaking of late..." Cici glances at her watch. "Where's Bianca?"

I roll my eyes and chuckle. "Cuban Time knows no limits. I gotta run, though. Tell her I love her when she gets here."

"She's gonna be jazzed about the billionaire." Meredith grins.

"Lil," Aubrey calls to me as I head toward the door. "Get this guy's business. We're already doing well, as you guys know from my weekly profit reports, but this...could be a game changer."

I toss my wavy, blonde ponytail over my shoulder and give a sassy shrug. "Consider it done, ladies. I'll be back!"

As I head down the hallway and into the elevator, I feel confidence and optimism propelling me forward...the very things that this business was built on. We've spent the last two years grinding and working and thriving—admittedly, having an absolute blast while doing it—and I've never let anything get in the way of this crazy dream.

Except, it's not a dream anymore. It's a reality. An accomplished, highly profitable reality that was made possible by hard work and positivity and friendship.

To be perfectly honest, I had no clue whether or not my wild and slightly drunk pipe dream of an idea would actually ever work out, but it's turned out to be a roaring success. We're businesswomen now, with a staff of over fifty people in our crew and some seriously high-profile clients.

And once Mr. Billionaire with a B signs up for our services, it's about to get even more high-profile. Maybe even enough to buy a bigger office space.

My heels click along the shiny, tan, marble floor of the lobby of our office building, my ponytail swinging back and forth as I hug my shoulder bag against me, triple-checking to make sure my iPad is in there.

"Oh, Florida," I whisper to myself as I step outside, the humidity hitting me hard even though it's November.

Feels like home.

I walk up to my BMW and get in, keying the address to this guy's Venetian Islands mansion into my GPS.

I feel...good. I feel put together and strong. I feel like I can take on the world.

As I follow the directions out to the islands, I go over my usual spiel in my head, whispering to myself possible answers to questions between sips of coffee.

As I cruise down the road, I glance to my right at the emerald-colored Biscayne Bay, glittering in the sunlight. I drive over the Venetian causeway, admiring the view of the islands, which are lush with greenery, bathed in sunshine, and covered in luxurious, jaw-dropping mansions.

Palm trees and sea grapes line the entrance to San Marino Island, where my new friend Theodore resides. I slow my speed as the road curves gently, lined with massive gates leading back to stunningly beautiful waterfront houses.

"House number three eighteen," I whisper to myself,

squinting into the sunlight to make out the house numbers on each gate and mailbox I pass.

There it is, 318.

The gate is open already, so I drive right through it, slowly making my way down a long driveway that crunches with shells and sand under my tires.

Finally, it turns into a big, round drive-up, with an elegant white fountain in the middle.

"Holy cow," I say under my breath, lifting my sunglasses onto my forehead as I crane my neck to see the house out of the car window.

It's everything a Miami Beach mansion should be. Painted a soft, pale orange with light red roof tiles, it's got more windows that I can count. Archways lead toward the enormous front door, which is entirely glass.

I step out of my car and lock it—not that that's necessary in this neighborhood—and try not to look too awestruck by the incredible home.

The façade of the house is complex and overwhelming, with alcoves and levels and multiple staircases. All I can see now are dollar signs when I think about what we can fairly charge to clean this place.

With a deep breath, I straighten my posture and knock on the front door.

My heart races a bit in my chest, but I know I can use the nerves and the jitters to fuel me, as I always do.

About a minute goes by with no answer, so I decide to knock again.

Nothing.

Huh. Maybe there's a doorbell I can ring...

I find the button for a doorbell on the side of the wall and press my finger down on it firmly.

Still no answer.

I glance at my phone. The time is 9:54. Well, I'm not late, but evidently Theodore is.

I guess I'm going to have to call and reschedule, but from what I remember this guy was insanely difficult to get a hold of, even after he reached out to us.

It could be weeks before we can set up another meeting, and I want this client *now*.

I look around the driveway, my high heels grinding on the sandy, red pavers. I brush off my black pencil skirt and the pink floral blouse I decided to wear, making sure everything still looks nice and neat and professional.

Meredith would be proud.

Okay, now I'm getting frustrated. Where the heck is this guy?

I spot a ritzy-looking Jaguar parked outside a garage on the other end of the circle driveway. So, *someone* has to be home.

He knew today was a consultation, right? He didn't think I was actually coming in to clean for the first time without getting everything set up in an initial meeting first, did he?

I whip out my phone and type a quick text to the girls in our Maid In Miami group chat.

So, I'm here. But he's not answering the door. Should I just take the loss and head back? I've tried knocking and ringing the bell, like, four times.

I let out a nervous breath and pace a bit as I wait for them to respond.

My phone buzzes with a text and I look at it instantly.

Aubrey Shepard: *Do you have his cell #? Might be worth giving him a call.*

I tap on my phone screen to open up the prospective client notes I have for Theodore Rinehart. The only number listed is his office phone number. Which I suppose I could try, but considering we had this consultation scheduled and his car is in the driveway, I doubt he's at the office.

My phone dings again.

Bianca Lopez: *Go peek around the house. Maybe he's out back or something.*

I snort and roll my eyes. I am not about to go snooping around a mansion looking for the billionaire owner. We'll just have to find a way to reschedule.

"Dammit," I grunt to myself, shaking my head with defeat as I head back down the driveway to my car.

As I'm walking, careful not to let my heels slip in the cracks between the pavers, I hear something rustling in the bushes alongside the driveway.

I stop in my tracks, my gaze darting to the source of the sound. "Hello?" I walk slowly and hesitantly toward the shrubbery. "Is someone there?"

Maybe's it's my guy! Or at least somebody who works for him who could tell me how I can get a hold of him.

I tiptoe toward the bushes, which are dense hibiscus plants dotted with bright pink flowers.

I don't hear any more sounds, so maybe it was just an animal, or the wind. It was awfully loud, though, to just have been a squirrel or something.

I step onto the grass and peek behind the dense bush,

and sure enough, I see a man bent down, fussing with something in the ground.

"Hey, hi, excuse me." I step gingerly over the grass and dirt, walking behind the bush, careful not to let my heels slip into the ground.

The man looks up, startled. "Can I help you with something?" A sudden low, masculine voice hits my ears and I step a bit closer.

"Oh!" I jump a little, my hands flying up to check my hair. "Sorry, I was just, uh...yes, actually, maybe you can."

He gets up and brushes off his knees, taking a couple of steps toward me.

My eyes do a quick and thorough scan of the man standing in front of me. Tall, with dark hair and a slightly scruffy five o'clock shadow over a chiseled jawline. Brown eyes dance as they meet my gaze, sending a shiver rippling through me. His tight white T-shirt hugs an impressively muscular body, accentuating bulging biceps and broad shoulders.

The shirt is smeared with soil and dirt and some green stains, and from the looks of it he's been sweating.

He must be the gardener. Or groundskeeper, or something.

Good, maybe he can help me get this guy's direct cell or a way to contact him.

I clear my throat and step back, straightening my shoulders and shaking off the sudden bullet train of attraction that just hit me.

I put a wide smile on my face and lift my chin. "I'm Lilly McCarthy, an owner of Maid In Miami, a high-end cleaning company here in the city. I had a consultation scheduled for today with Theodore Rinehart..." I cock my head, waiting for him to respond and at least let me know I'm at the right house.

He wipes his hands on the already-filthy shirt and gives a crooked smile. "Hi, Lilly."

"Hi." I swallow the tingly sparky feeling that his smile just induced and stay professional. "I'm sorry to be snooping around in the bushes here; I just heard you and I'm really looking for any way I could possibly be able to get in touch with Theodore. Since you work for him, too, maybe you can give me his direct cell number?"

He inches back a little, a new kind of smile playing at his sexy mouth. He narrows his gaze, drinking me in like a glass of lemonade in the middle of July.

Suddenly conscious of my appearance, I inhale sharply.

He just keeps his gaze locked with mine, smiling as if he's almost fighting a laugh, but is also completely enamored with me.

I have to admit the enamored feeling is pretty mutual.

"Do you...have his cell?" I ask softly. "You're the gardener, right? I mean, do you report directly to him, or..."

For a couple beats, he studies my face, then nods his head quickly and gives an easy laugh. "Yeah, I'm the, uh, I'm the gardener. And, you know, Theodore is actually not here right now, he...had to run to the office for something urgent."

"Oh, okay." I brush a pesky flyaway behind my ear and shift in my heels. "Well, maybe I can just send him an email or something; it's just that's he's very hard to reach sometimes, and I'd really love to—"

"I can tell him you stopped by," Hot Gardener says quickly.

"Would you?" I look up at him and grin, noticing the way his hair falls around his forehead, just barely brushing the tops of his defined brows. "That would be amazing."

"Yeah, for sure." He lifts a shoulder. "I'll tell him to give you a call. Or, better yet, send you an email, so everything can be in writing."

"Wow, thank you." I laugh as happiness and relief swell in my chest. "Thank you so much. Oh! I didn't get your name?"

"TJ," he says slowly, holding my gaze firm and steady. "I'm TJ."

"Well, you've been so helpful, TJ. Thank you."

"Anytime. I'd shake your hand but mine are covered in dirt." He chuckles and shakes his head. "I've been trying to fix this sprinkler back behind the hibiscus plants; it's a real problem."

I give a soft laugh. "I would imagine you're pretty used to getting your hands dirty. Par for the course with your line of work."

He bends down again, twisting at the black, plastic sprinkler knob in the ground.

Suddenly, it starts shooting water out in all directions, soaking both of us.

"Oh!" I shriek and leap back, my blouse practically drenched and my hair dripping.

"Oh, my God. I am so sorry," TJ calls at me over the humming sound of the spraying water. "I don't know how to...." He messes with the sprinkler some more, getting absolutely drenched in the process.

I leap out of the splash zone and wipe myself off, laughing through the shock and ridiculousness of it. My electronics are fine, and my outfit will survive; the only thing I can focus on at this particular moment is his now see-through T-shirt and dripping wet hair.

"Come on," he grunts at the sprinkler, fiddling with it until it finally stops spraying.

"I'm really sorry about that..." TJ stands up, holding up a hand apologetically. His whole body is soaked, and I can see the outlines of his muscles through the shirt. Water droplets fall off of his nose and chin, and he smiles at me.

"It's totally fine." I shake my head and laugh. "I'll dry off. I got away pretty quickly, so I was mostly spared." I glance down at the huge wet blob on my blouse and skirt. "Mostly."

"I feel terrible." He cocks his head.

"It's okay, really. I can stop at my apartment and get a change of clothes before going back to the office."

"You sure I can't get you anything?"

"It's fine, I promise." I sling my bag over my shoulder and step out onto the driveway, turning back to give him a teasing look. "You're not a very good gardener, though." I wink playfully.

Something glimmers in his eyes as he stifles a smile, biting his lip and glancing down at the ground. "I have my moments. Well, it was wonderful to meet you, Lilly. And I'm so sorry about the sprinkler incident."

"Pleasure was all mine." My voice comes out a bit more flirtatious than I would have liked it to but...whatever. "And don't forget to talk to Theodore for me. Assuming I get his business, I guess I'll be seeing a lot more of you."

He gives me a big thumbs up as I head back to my car and hit unlock. "I'd like that."

I give a soft, easy laugh and wipe a drop of water that falls down my cheek. "I'd like that, too."

I slide into the driver's seat and do my best to bite back my smile until I'm at least down the driveway.

I may be soaked with sprinkler water, and I may not have met the old, rich prospective client just yet, but this morning was most definitely not wasted.

TWO

TJ

Why did I do that? Why did I let that sweet, gorgeous, charming girl believe I was the *gardener* that entire conversation? Why didn't I correct her? Why couldn't I find the willpower to open my mouth and say, "Theodore Rinehart? Oh, yes. That's me. *I'm* Theodore Rinehart, but everyone calls me TJ. I own this house, and I'm the person you're looking for. The billionaire, the hedge fund manager."

No, no. My brilliant and totally reasonable brain decides to go with, "Why yes, I am the gardener and I'll talk to Theodore for you." Which should be very easy, considering I am literally him.

But, no. Instead of being honest and correcting her very valid and reasonable—if entirely wrong—assumption, I decide to keep the lie going and add insult to injury by soaking her with this stupid faulty sprinkler.

She's right. I'm a terrible gardener. Because I'm not a

gardener, I'm a hedge fund manager. And I came down to Miami and bought this place so I'd have somewhere to get away from New York's cold winters and even colder people.

She's one of the first people I've met since arriving here, and she was just about the furthest thing from cold. A swinging blonde ponytail, gigantic, intoxicating blue eyes, and an outfit that perfectly toed the line between business and pleasure.

I decide to give up on the sprinkler and call someone else to come and fix it. An actual gardener. Heading into my new house, I shield my eyes from the blistering sun and wipe droplets of sweat from my forehead. In November? Seriously?

I sure am far from NYC. And I honestly couldn't be happier about it.

The house is big and open, with an awesome view of the bay. It feels like a tropical resort—nothing like my glass skybox of a penthouse that overlooks Central Park. The whole back of the house is floor to ceiling windows, with sunlight pouring in and bouncing off the light marble floors. There's a curved staircase on either side of the entryway, making it feel even more like a resort.

Having always bounced around Manhattan apartments, I've never had a place of this size to myself. So, I knew one of the first things I had to do was find a solid cleaning service. I want to hire as few people to work at this house as possible, because I really came here for privacy and solitude more than anything.

But I sure am glad I found her. Even though she's going

to think I'm a total jerk when she finds out I'm not the gardener but, in fact, the billionaire.

Taking a deep breath, I push open the sliding glass doors in the back of the entryway, stepping out into the breathtaking backyard. The Miami skyline glistens across the water, accented by yachts and boats floating on the water, and the backdrop of a clear, blue sky.

Why didn't I tell her?

I think about this for a second, leaning against the doorframe and taking in the newness and extravagance of my change of scenery.

I don't know why I didn't tell her. I guess there was just something so refreshing about having a woman look at me without *knowing*. Having a woman—or anyone, really—look at me and see anything but money is rare these days.

I've been burned more than a few times by girls who are enchanted by the money instead of me. They get infatuated with the lifestyle they think I could give them, instead of the actual man that I am.

Hence...I'm single. Very, *very* single. And the first truly positive and exciting interaction I've had with a woman in quite some time was only so great because she thought I was the freaking gardener.

Nice going, TJ.

It just gets old. The money, the status, the wealth...it feels like that's all people see. But not Lilly. She just saw *me*. With no pretense or assumptions. Without the weight of my job and my net worth completely clouding her impression of me. She just thinks I'm a crappy gardener.

I smile a little at the thought, looking down at the damp T-shirt clinging to my skin.

I yank it off and drape it over the back of a patio chair to dry, before heading back inside and pulling the glass slider shut.

My office sits at the end of a long hallway off of the entrance to the house, and it's the only room I've already completely set up and moved into. I spend more time there than anywhere else, especially since I'm doing ninety percent of my work remotely when I'm down here in Miami.

I walk through the big, white double doors that lead into the bright and airy office space. My desk sits in the center of the room, and tall bookshelves anchor each corner behind it. Huge windows let in tons of light and even more glances of the breathtakingly tropical view.

With a sigh, I sit down at my desk, wiggling the mouse to wake up my iMac.

I've got to get to work. And I've really got to get that spunky blonde charmer out of my head. Well, I did tell her I'd have "Theodore" send her an email...

Before reopening any of my work tabs and documents, I go to my personal email that I had used to originally correspond with Maid In Miami to hire a cleaning service.

I start typing up a draft.

Hello, Lilly. This is Theodore Rinehart. First of all, I think it's probably important that I tell you something before we get into business details. We actually met this morning, when you came over for a consultation. You thought I was the gardener, and I didn't correct you, but I actually am Theodore, the owner of the house. Sorry if this seems

I stare at the screen and draw a blank. Chewing on my

lip, I rest my head in my hands and run a finger through my still slightly damp hair.

My mind keeps flashing with images of her, the way she looked at me. No judgement or preconceived ideas or expectations about who I am and how I act. Just...me. She wasn't nervous or intimidated or going out of her way to impress me. She wasn't putting on some sort of fake persona that she thinks a "rich guy" will like, the way so many girls who meet me do.

There was something so endearing, amusing, *captivating* about her adorably naïve mistake. And the anonymity was insanely refreshing.

I slowly hover my fingers over the keyboard, lightly tapping backspace over and over again until the email just says:

Hello, Lilly. This is Theodore Rinehart.

I swallow and keep typing. Just for fun. I'm not gonna send it.

My groundskeeper, TJ, mentioned that you stopped by this morning. My sincerest apologies for missing our meeting; I got caught up in the office much longer than I had anticipated. No need to reschedule a consultation, I am more than ready to go ahead and move forward. I'd like to hire you and have your team come to the house to clean twice a week. Does next Monday sound like a good start date? Thank you.

I lean back in my desk chair and scan the email, shaking my head and laughing softly to myself.

I'm not gonna send it. I'm not gonna keep up some silly charade of this false identity. I should just delete it and come clean. It was an honest mistake on her part, and as soon as I tell her the truth, she'll...

See me exactly the same way that everyone else does.

The thought makes me wince, and on a completely unhinged moment of impulse, I set my hand down on the mouse and click send.

"Oh, crap," I mutter to myself, watching the email shoot off into cyberspace.

I drop my head into my hands, laughing in disbelief. I just got myself deeper into this lie.

But is it really a lie? I didn't personally come up with it. It's not like I walked up to her and said, "Hey, I'm the gardener."

I just didn't *correct* her when she said it. Is that the same as lying?

Either way, I'm weirdly excited to see her again.

As *the gardener*.

THREE

LILLY

"I have good news and I have bad news," I announce, striding back into the tiny office in fresh, dry clothes with a smile on my face.

Meredith lifts her gaze and smiles at me with her huge doe-eyes. "Bad news first. Get it over with."

"No, good news first!" Bianca insists, looking up from over her laptop screen and raising her brows. Her desk is directly across from Meredith's, with the rest of us placed around them.

"Why would you do good news first?" Aubrey asks on a laugh, tapping something on her keyboard.

"It softens the blow of the bad news." Bianca sips a coffee and shrugs. "Duh."

"Okay, okay." I hold up my hands and squeeze through the tight arrangement of desks to get to mine back in the corner. "The bad news is that I didn't meet with the billionaire."

"What? Why?" Cici's dark eyes widen and she tilts her head.

"Dang..." Bianca shakes her head. "After you texted us for advice, we didn't hear from you again, so we all kind of assumed you eventually ended up finding your way to Mr. Moneybags."

"Not quite." I sit down in my small, white leather desk chair and scoot it forward to reach my computer.

"Wait a minute..." Meredith narrows her gaze, studying me. "Did you change? I could have sworn you were wearing pink this morning."

"Uh, yes, I had to run home and change. But I'll get to that." I laugh dryly.

"Goodness girl, you've had yourself quite a morning." Cici laughs.

"No kidding." I push a strand of hair that escaped my ponytail back behind my ear and lean forward to continue. "So, right when I was about to just throw in the towel and give up on my meeting with the billionaire, I stumbled upon the gardener who works at the house. He was messing with a sprinkler behind some bushes."

"As gardeners do," Aubrey adds.

"Right. So I figured he might be my only shot to at least talk to *someone*."

Meredith eyes me. "Please tell me you didn't go trekking through the bushes hunting down the gardener to ask him about the rich guy."

"Oh, but I did. And I'm very glad I did." I straighten my shoulders and sit up confidently. "Because not only did he promise to speak directly to Theodore and tell him to get in contact with me ASAP, he was also..." I feel a laugh bubble in my chest as I dramatically fan myself. "*Totally hot.*"

"Hah!" Bianca snorts.

"Oh my gosh, Lil." Aubrey chuckles and rolls her eyes.

"I'm serious, you guys. This man was, like, Grade A fine. All sweaty and dirty and...mmm!" I dramatically fan myself. "I haven't been so instantly attracted to someone in ages. It was electric."

"Nothing like a sweaty, dirty man." Cici nods her head and looks longingly out the window. "Why do you think I'm such a sucker for athletes?"

Meredith laughs and shakes her head. "I like clean men."

"You just haven't met the right messy, gritty, down and dirty guy." Bianca arches a brow at Meredith.

"I think I prefer my men not dirty," Meredith insists. "Is that such a crime?"

"How do you know what you prefer, *Virgin Mer-y?*" Cici teases her gently and nudges her playfully from across her desk.

"Oh, shut it, all of yous." Meredith waves her hands. "I have absolutely no shame in the fact that I'm still a virgin."

"And you shouldn't," Bianca says sweetly. "We love who you are."

"We do, Mer," I agree, smiling. "But speaking of getting in bed with someone...I'd like to. With the gardener."

"Ah, yes, back to the gardener." Aubrey points at me. "Finish your story."

I shrug. "That's really all there is to it. We had a...

moment. And he said he'd tell Theodore to email me, which was really nice of him, and that was about it."

"Okay, but..." Meredith frowns. "None of that explains the change of clothes."

"Oh, right!" I laugh, glancing down at my fresh outfit. "When he was trying to fix the sprinkler, it sort of sprayed...everywhere. It completely soaked me. And him. So I stopped at home on my way back here to change and clean up."

"No freaking way," Bianca chokes on a laugh.

"He definitely did that on purpose." Aubrey taps the side of her head.

"Either that or he's a *really* crappy gardener," Meredith adds.

"That's what I said!" I shake the mouse on my desk, waking up my computer screen to check my email. "Anyway, it was just a funny little encounter. I doubt anything will come of it, although I imagine I'll be seeing this guy a good bit if we're both working at the same house."

"Maybe next time he'll 'accidentally' push you in the pool." Cici winks playfully.

"What was his name?" Aubrey asks.

"TJ." I glance at her. "No clue what it stands for, though."

"Terrible Jerk," Meredith supplies quickly.

I laugh and roll my eyes. "He was not. At all."

"Trustworthy Janitor," Bianca adds, raising her hand.

Cici chimes in. "Total Jock."

Aubrey gasps and widens her gaze ominously. "The Joker."

We all laugh as I wave off their silly comments. "Let's

just hope The Joker gets his elusive boss to...oh!" As if spoken into existence, my email inbox refreshes with a new message from Theodore Rinehart.

"What?" Aubrey asks eagerly. "Did he email?"

"He sure did." I grin widely, scanning the words fast and whispering them to myself as I read through the message.

"And?" The girls all stare at me in anticipation.

"Yes!" I pump my fist with victory. "He said he doesn't even need a consultation, he wants our team to come in and clean twice a week starting on Monday!"

"Woohoo!" Cici claps her hands.

"That's what I'm talking about," Bianca cheers.

"A house that size..." Aubrey shakes her head slowly, her smile widening as she processes the news. "With the quality of furnishings and materials..."

"We can charge a fortune," I say. "And rightfully so. It's going to be a thorough and intensive job, so we'll want to bring our most experienced crew members onto this job."

"Diana is the best with the super, super high-end stuff." Aubrey scrolls through her computer screen. "She knows about chemicals and reactions and what's safe to use on really expensive surfaces. Bring her and her daughter, Leah, for sure. I'll look through the rest of the staff and come up with a team."

"You guys..." Meredith stands up, holding her arms out. "We got our first billionaire."

"We got our first billionaire!" I jump up and give all my best friends tight hugs, squeezing them as we laugh and celebrate.

Pride and happiness echo through me, and I can't stop smiling with the feeling of success.

Well, it's mostly the success that's making me smile. It's only a little bit because I know I'm going to be seeing TJ the Gardener again on Monday.

FOUR

TJ

I GLANCE THROUGH THE WINDOW OF MY OFFICE, which looks out at the round driveway that circles around the front of the house.

I see a big van pull up, painted light pink with a cute, animated Maid In Miami logo across the side.

Shoot. She's here.

I have to tell her. I have to just come clean and be real about who I am and accept the fact that she's probably going to never come here again.

I lean back in my chair and crane my neck a bit to get a better view in between the white slats of the plantation shutters.

Four women pile out of the van, each carrying different cleaning supplies and materials.

And then...there's Lilly. Dressed more casual for her on-site work, she's got on faded jeans and a Maid In Miami

T-shirt. She's wearing bright white sneakers and that same adorably bouncy ponytail she had the other day.

She's holding an iPad, smiling and chatting with the cleaning crew, gesturing at different parts of the house from the outside.

I wonder if she's expecting to see the gardener. Well, she's about to. Sort of.

The knock on the front door breaks my train of thought, and I quickly jump up, shut my laptop, and walk out of the office.

Without really thinking about it, I shut the heavy, white wood doors to the office and lock them with the keys in my pocket, deadbolting that room shut. It doesn't need much cleaning, anyway.

I head down the long hallway and swing the door open, swallowing an unfamiliar tingle of nerves.

"Oh!" Lilly jolts back, her blue eyes widening as a smile pulls. "It's...you."

I suck in a breath and shrug. "It's me."

"I just thought you'd be..." She glances over her shoulder at the mangrove bush where the unforgettable sprinkler accident happened. "Outside."

"Well, actually I..." I pause, looking at her. The vibrant determination on her face sending electricity through her expression.

She gazes at me, not trying to hide her own attraction.

I clear my throat and jut my chin back toward the kitchen. "I just came in for a water break. Theodore...isn't here."

The lie tastes a tad bitter, but I decide quickly and

impulsively to just follow my gut. Just for a second. Just for a little.

"Oh, okay." She smiles brightly, thankfully not noticing that I don't seem to have a drop of sweat or smudge of dirt anywhere on me. "Well, this is my crew." Lilly turns around and introduces the women behind her. "Diana, Leah, Kristi, and Beth."

I nod and wave at the women.

"This is TJ," Lilly continues confidently. "He's the gardener."

"Nice to meet you all." I offer easy smiles to the cleaning crew.

They exchange pleasantries in return, and Lilly tilts her chin back up to meet my gaze, fire sparking behind her eyes. "You sure he's not here?"

He's standing right in front of you.

"Positive." I raise my brows apologetically. "But I'm sure it's fine if you guys go ahead and get started. I'm pretty sure he wanted your team to just jump on in."

She walks past me into the entryway, gesturing for her crew to head into the house and start getting a feel for it. "He told you that?" She tips her head.

"Oh, um, yeah he..." I scratch the back of my neck, realizing suddenly I'm going to have to become a slightly better liar if I have any intention of keeping this up. "He mentioned it."

"Oh." Lilly nods, her focus quickly shifting to the house around her and away from me. "Well, thank you so much for talking to him." She looks over her shoulder and gives me a sweet smile. "I really appreciate it."

"Yeah, no worries," I say, a bit sheepishly. "Oh, one

thing I should tell you though, he keeps his office locked when he's not home. I guess it's his...personal space. So you can probably just stay out of that room."

"Huh..." Lilly considers this for a second before quickly rolling her eyes and giving a shrug. "Rich business people. Between you and me...they're all weirdos," she whispers with a soft giggle, leaning close enough to give me a jolt.

I force a laugh. "You're not wrong."

And she's not. Considering that I, a rich business person, am currently pretending to be a gardener so she doesn't know who I really am, I'd say I definitely fall under the category of weirdo. Or lunatic, even.

"Well, I'll let you get back to the landscaping." She straightens her shoulders and holds my gaze. "I'm gonna give myself a little house tour and get some specs for estimates."

"Right, sounds good. And just let me know if you need anything, I'm—" I catch myself quickly, trying to play it off. "I'm pretty sure I'm the only one here, so..."

"Gotcha. Thanks, TJ." Her eyes linger on mine, and I let my gaze slide down her beautiful face. Smooth, rosy cheeks and the sweetest heart-shaped lips I've ever seen. It's framed with wisps and strands of silky blonde hair that got out of the ponytail and are falling around her gorgeous features.

Before I get too carried away and let my gaze continue further south down her incredible body, I give a nod and a half-smile. "Anytime."

While she walks through the house, noting things on her tablet, making phone calls to her business partners, and coming up with plans with her housekeeping crew, I walk outside to the backyard, pretending to be the gardener.

Well, I'll use it as an excuse to get some fresh air, at least. I've been at my desk since six this morning, so it's actually nice to be in the sun. The weather, after all, is why I'm down here.

Or at least that's what I told everyone and what I've been telling myself. But the reality is...I needed an escape. A break. Not from the work itself, but from the culture of it. The status, the money, the elite people...it got to be sickening and exhausting. Once I found out I could do everything remotely, I closed on this house within a week.

And maybe that's why I'm so drawn to the idea of a woman who doesn't know who I am. It's not real. It's not serious. It's an *escape*.

I wander out into the lush area of the backyard, between the giant pool deck and the actual bay. The water is deep blue and totally calm, still underneath the blistering sun. The air is clear and warm and salty with a slight breeze, reminding me of vacations.

I meander through the sea grapes and mangroves, wondering what gardening I could actually do. I mean, might as well be productive while I'm out here.

"Holy moly!" A sweet, musical voice startles me and I look up from my fake plant study.

Lilly walks through the slider and looks around, taking in the backyard and its magnificent view. She catches sight of me and walks over, smiling and shaking her head. "This backyard is absolutely insane. I've seen a lot of beautiful properties in Miami, but this..." She gestures her arm back and forth at the glittering Biscayne Bay. "This just might take the cake."

"It's beautiful, isn't it?" I agree, cocking my head as I walk closer to her.

"Stunning. Well, they're all set and cleaning already, so I'm just in supervising mode for now." She taps the iPad.

"Do you supervise every job?" I ask, thanking the universe for the bead of sweat I feel on my forehead so it actually sort of looks like I've been doing some kind of work out here.

"No, but one of us does. Well, every big job. The high-profile clients." She toys with a pink flower in her fingers.

"You have business partners, I take it." I sit down on a white wooden bench that overlooks the water view, silently inviting her to join me.

She sits down, brushing off her jeans. "I do. But they're not just business partners. They're my best friends. The five of us started Maid In Miami after we finished getting our MBAs at UF. We had no idea what to do with our lives—any of us—but I had crafted a business plan for a high-end cleaning company as my final business school project and, voilà. Maid In Miami was born."

I laugh dryly, leaning my elbows on my thighs and tipping my head to meet her gaze. "A final project? You're kidding."

"Not at all. We decided to just take the chance, however crazy it seemed. Now, we all co-own the company. And it's been very successful," she says, the hint of pride and confidence in her voice only making me more drawn to her.

"Well, congratulations, Lilly," I say, sincerity in my voice.

She smiles at me, her eyes beaming. "Thank you. I'm really proud of everything my friends and I have accomplished. We had to work for it, you know? Actually build something from the ground up. People like..." She gestures vaguely at the house and the pool and the backyard. "People like *this* who just get millions of dollars handed to them..." She rolls her eyes and makes a face. "They don't get it."

I swallow and glance down at my feet, really conflicted about how and when and if I should mention who I am.

"Yeah," I mutter, clenching my jaw a little. "I know what you mean."

"Like the elusive Theodore," she says on a laugh, mocking her idea of the owner of this house and what he's probably like. "Just lucked out that his daddy had a hedge fund and money coming out of his ears and voilà! Life of luxury." She shakes her head, glancing at me. "I can't stand people who just get handouts like that. I believe in hard work. People like...us."

I suck in a sharp breath and meet her gaze. Her twinkling blue eyes admire me, and I'm pretty sure this is the first time in my life I've ever been admired by a woman because she thinks I'm...

Not rich?

"You're a special woman, Lilly." I bite my lip and hold her gaze, enchanted by the depth of her eyes and the genuine *realness* in her expression and words.

She laughs softly, lifting a shoulder. "What do you mean? You hardly know me."

"Yeah, but..." I run a hand through my hair and squint up at the blinding sun, thinking about what to say. "I can just tell. There's not a lot of girls who think like you. Plus you're driven, motivated, smart..." I lean closer to her, almost close enough to hear her heartbeat. "Beautiful," I say under my breath.

Her soft, pink lips are slightly parted, and every single cell in my body is begging me to kiss them. And she isn't exactly pulling away either.

I came to Florida on an impulse. Maybe impulse is my new thing.

I lean in to kiss her, the world drowned out with nothing but the quiet calm of the water and the whisper of the breeze. Just as my lips are an inch from hers—

"Lilly?" A voice calls from far away, and we both jolt back and jump away from each other, rattled.

Lilly stands up quickly and brushes herself off, straightening her shoulders.

"Lilly..." The voice gets closer, and I see Diana, one of her cleaning crew members, walking around the hedges looking for her. "Hey, we just had a question about the grout in the tile of the upstairs bathroom. We weren't sure if we should—"

"I'll go take a look at it!" she says quickly and cheerfully, but I can tell she's still reeling from what just happened.

Well, what *almost* happened.

She glances back at me and our gazes lock for a split second, some sort of silent communication reverberating between us.

"Diana, I'll..." She looks back at me and then to Diana again. "I'll meet you up there in, like, two minutes."

Diana, blessedly oblivious, gives two thumbs up and turns around to head back into the house. "Sounds good."

After a beat or two of deafening silence, we both start laughing and shaking our heads, sighing with relief and surprise and letting the awkward tension melt away.

"Would you, um—" Here I go...impulse again. "Would you wanna have dinner with me? Or a drink? Or...ice cream?" I stand up from the bench as I ask the question, meeting her face to face.

Lilly laughs, bubbly and sweet, twirling her ponytail as she considers my offer. "Going on a date with a fellow employee at this house..." She raises a brow teasing me. "A bit scandalous, don't you think?"

Not as scandalous as going on a date with the billionaire you're working for.

"I'm kidding." She grins. "I'd love to." She reaches into her pocket and pulls out a business card, decorated with the same pink design as the side of the van. "Here's my number."

As if I don't already have it.

"Great." I give an easy smile, tapping the card on my other hand. "I'll call you."

She glances over her shoulder as she bounces away, back toward the house. "I'll answer."

I can't tell her. I *should* tell her. But...man. I don't want to tell her. At all.

It's not like it's going to be something serious or long-term, right? No way. It's just...a fantasy. It's the first time in my life I get to just be TJ, and have someone see me without the filters and lenses and assumptions that have always followed me around.

This whole winter home in Miami was supposed to be an escape for me. A little isolated bubble...far, far away from reality and my life in New York City. Maybe she can just be part of that escape. Maybe...for once...I can just feel *normal*. Before I have to go back to my real world.

Just, for once, I want to know what it feels like to be with a girl who doesn't look at me and see dollar signs.

And I'll go back to reality soon enough, but for right now, I need this escape. I need this freedom and time away from it all.

And she just seems to fit right into that.

FIVE

LILLY

Laughter, music, and the hum of happy conversation fills the air of Coconuts, our favorite bar in the entire city, and our go-to for every imaginable occasion, even when there isn't one.

The bar sits on a third-floor rooftop, with an indoor section and an outdoor section. Its beachside location makes the whole aesthetic feel warm and salty and beachy. String lights hang all across the roof, twinkling as people dance and drink and laugh underneath them. Everything here is decorated with a tropical, tiki theme, the drinks are cheap, the food is fabulous, and the environment just never gets old.

The five of us have been sitting at the same corner section along the bar since we graduated business school and sat right in this very spot nailing down every detail of Maid In Miami.

"Wait, wait, wait..." Meredith waves her hand, sipping

something sweet and frozen, a typical Meredith drink. "He asked you *out*? Like on a real date?"

"I didn't even know people did that anymore," Aubrey remarks, shaking her head.

"Seriously," Bianca muses. "I thought everything was just swipe left, swipe right, Netflix and chill..."

We all laugh at this, and I look down at my gin and tonic, stirring it with the straw. "No swiping, no Netflix and chill. The hot gardener from the billionaire's house asked me on a real, old-fashioned date." I sit up straight, proudly.

"Look at you, girl." Cici shoves me playfully.

"It's about time one of us has some sort of romance," Bianca says. "We've all been working our cute little booties off since graduation and not a single one of us has really had a man."

"Not for lack of trying, on your part," Aubrey teases Bianca, subtly nodding her head toward Alec, the mysterious and handsome bartender who's been working here longer than we've been coming here. Bianca's had a soul-melting crush on him and flirts with him at every imaginable turn, but he's just about the only guy in the world that doesn't reciprocate her flirty energy. And it drives her *crazy*. Which we all, of course, think is hilarious.

"I wouldn't say I *have* a man." I hold up a finger cautiously. "I'm...in talks with a man."

Meredith giggles and sips her frozen fruity thing. "Very exciting, Lil."

"When's the date?" Aubrey asks, leaning her elbow on the bar as she turns to the side to face me.

"Friday night, I think." I shrug my shoulders and swirl

my drink around, trying to hide my smile. "It's just dinner, you guys."

"Those rosy pink cheeks of yours are saying it's more than just dinner," Cici teases me, pinching my cheek.

"I mean...I don't know. I've only met the guy twice. He could still be anyone at this point. An axe murderer, even."

"Oh, please." Bianca rolls her eyes.

Aubrey, the only person in the world who would take that comment even remotely seriously, widens her gaze and leans toward me. "Make sure you have your location shared with all of us when you go. Just in case."

However silly, my heart is warmed by the sentiment. "I promise, Aub."

"Well this is all very exciting." Meredith grins brightly and raises her glass.

Bianca raises hers, too. "Tonight, we celebrate our first billionaire client, and Lilly's love affair with the gardener."

I snort and roll my eyes as we all tap our drinks together and take a sip.

"You ladies good over here? Need another round?" The husky voice of the always-busy bartender, Alec, breaks through our chatty celebration.

He leans over the bar, eyeing Bianca just enough to make her melt with a crush, but not enough to show actual interest.

"Yeah..." Bianca says slowly, a flirty smile playing at the corners of her mouth as she lets her gaze slide over him. "We'll do another round."

"Oh, no." Meredith waves her hand and shakes her head. "I'm good."

Cici laughs. "You've had half a piña colada, Mer."

"What?" Meredith taps her glass. "These are strong. Aren't they, Alec?"

He gives a low chuckle as he pours more drinks for us, smoothly grazing the liquor bottles over the tops of each glass. "Yeah. Strong with sugar."

Meredith lifts a shoulder. "Well, I like it."

"You're unapologetically yourself, Meredith." Alec smiles sweetly as he passes out the drinks to the other four of is. "In fact, all of you are that way."

I swear his gaze lingers on Bianca for a second before he heads off to help some other customers.

"Did you guys see that?" she exclaims as soon as he's out of earshot, her dark eyes giant and wide.

Aubrey slowly raises her brows and gives an easy laugh. "See...what?"

"He totally wants me."

"B..." Aubrey says. "We've been frequent regulars here for over two years now. I think you might need to set your sights elsewhere."

"Yeah," Cici agrees, playing with the straw in her drink. "There's something...secretive about him. Something that makes me think there's a whole lot more to that guy than mixing drinks."

"Exactly," Bianca insists. "And I want to know what it is."

"Making judgmental comments is probably part of it." Meredith wrinkles her nose, defensively clutching her piña colada.

"Not the nicest guy in the world, that Alec," I agree. "But he's an intriguing one."

"I like 'em mean." Bianca lifts a shoulder.

"Not as intriguing as"—Cici grins widely at me and flicks her brows—"*the gardener.*"

"I doubt anything is going to come of this, you guys. Seriously." I push a strand of hair behind my ear. "We work together. Well, sort of. Besides, I'm way too busy for a relationship."

Aubrey makes a face. "I smell a cop out."

"Seriously, Lil." Meredith reaches over and touches my arm. "Don't just run away from this and use work as an excuse. He could be awesome. This could be really good."

"Yeah, for real." Bianca glances at me. "What happened to you, Miss Optimism?"

"I don't know, I..." I puff out a breath, thinking about this. "I guess I'm a bit less optimistic when it comes to the whole realm of dating. You know, ever since..."

I don't even have to say the name Aaron before all of my friends silently nod and acknowledge the heartbreak they all watched me endure the first semester of business school, when my boyfriend of three years decided to sleep with a college freshman.

The thought still makes me cringe a little.

"I get it." Aubrey places her hand on mine. "Trauma and heartbreak and broken trust are not easy things to get over. It only makes sense that you'd be cautious."

"I learned the cautious thing from you," I tease her, lightening the mood a bit. "But, yeah. As you all know, I haven't been serious with anyone since him." I pause for a second and swallow. "I haven't even been *casual* with anyone since him."

"He was gross." Meredith frowns.

"Scum of the earth," Cici adds.

"We're proud of you for putting yourself back out there, seriously." Bianca gives a bright, genuine smile and nudges me.

"Thanks, guys."

As we sip drinks and tease each other and laugh the rest of the evening, my mind wanders off, toying with the possibilities of what could come from my date with TJ.

I guess it wouldn't come as a surprise to anyone that I have a *very* good feeling about it.

SIX

TJ

"SHE FIRED THE NANNY, *AGAIN*?" I LAUGH AND SWIRL my beer around in the glass, looking across the table at two of my good friends, Blake Washington and Dominic Lowry.

Two of my best buds from Cornell, both of them ended up working in the same network of financial investment companies that I'm involved with, and they're two of the only guys I know very well here in Miami. After getting a little stir crazy by myself in the new house, I decided to link up with them and grab a beer.

"Yes. Three." Blake raises his brows and gestures his hands for emphasis. "That's three nannies that my wife has gone through in the last month."

Dominic turns to him and narrows his gaze. "Cheyenne is a picky woman."

"That she is." Blake shrugs. "But, I love her. And little

Grace deserves the best, so, can't argue with her wanting perfection."

"How old is Grace now?" I ask.

"Thirteen months." Blake smiles, his expression softening at the thought of his first baby. He reaches down for his phone and holds it up to show me a picture. "I know I've sent you all of these and posted them everywhere imaginable but, still. I can't get enough."

"Happy for you, man." I give an easy laugh and take a sip from my beer glass. "Dom, how are you and Angie?"

"Good, dude, really good." He nods. "We're in the thick of the wedding planning so...you know how that goes. Tasting hors d'oeuvres and cake samples and picking out flower arrangements." He rolls his eyes and tilts his head back. "It's never ending."

"I can imagine." I chuckle, shaking my head and tamping down the tiniest whisper of envy that nags at the corner of my mind. "It's so great to see you guys, seriously."

"Dang right it is." Blake reaches across the table to give me a fist bump. "When you said you were buying a house down here, I was so stoked."

"Three musketeers back at it." Dom laughs.

"Kappa Tau Omega for life," I say jokingly with a laugh, shaking my head at the thousands of memories I shared with these guys over the four years of college.

Truth be told, after so long of being surrounded by stuffy, uptight Manhattan elites, it feels good to just relax with my college boys like old times.

"What about you, TJ?" Dominic nudges my arm. "Still flying solo?"

"Seriously?" Blake asks, leaning forward eagerly before

I have a chance to even answer. "Bro, there's no way you're still completely single."

I raise my hands defensively. "Guilty, I guess."

"Get outta here." Blake leans back in his chair and laughs dryly, studying me. "But you're Theodore Rinehart Junior."

"Billionaire," Dominic adds with exaggerated emphasis. "How are you not wifed up?"

"Girls always were chasing you." Blake swirls his beer, chuckling. "Even back in college, they followed you around and fan-girled."

I lift a shoulder and laugh it off. "They just knew who my dad was, that's all."

"Uh, yeah." Dominic furrows his brow. "Exactly. One of the major perks of coming from money."

I swallow my disagreement.

Blake juts his chin. "And women loved me because they knew who my great-great-great-great-grandfather was."

"Oh my God, not this again," I groan and roll my eyes, stifling laughter.

"He's still on this," Dominic says to me, pointing at Blake. "Somehow, he's still on this."

"I told you guys," Blake says insistently. "I'm related to George Washington."

Dominic turns to Blake, pressing his hands together and shoving them into Blake's chest. "No. You are not."

"You guys are just haters." He finishes a beer and laughs easily.

"It's a common last name," Dom asserts.

"Not that common."

"Prove it," I say on a laugh. "Do one of those ancestry kits and show us the results."

Blake waves off the comment and shakes his head. "I don't need that. I know George's DNA is in my blood. I can feel it."

"Good God." Dom holds his palm to his forehead. "Okay, back to Mr. Celibacy, over here."

I grunt and run a hand through my hair.

"You're not seeing anyone? Even casually?"

I suck in a breath and let it out slowly, glancing out the window of the restaurant and bar we're at. It's a bougie kind of place on Brickell, the bottom of a glass skyscraper in the nicest area of the city. It's got outdoor dining with fancy looking ivy and trellises and arches everywhere, but we're sitting inside by the bar.

"Well, I haven't in a while, but I did meet someone actually, a few days ago…"

"There it is." Blake points a finger at me.

"See? Miami girls are just different, aren't they?"

I laugh softly and raise a shoulder. "I guess so, because the one I've met I already vibe with way more than any chick I went out with in New York. We're going out Friday night."

"Nice, nice. Love to hear it." Blake smiles. "How'd you meet her?"

"Does she work at your company?" Dom asks. "Oh, wait, no. You said you're fully remote down here."

"Yeah, I am. No, she doesn't work for me. It's, uh…" I glance out at the view of the glittery skyline and jungle of glass buildings. "Kind of a funny story, actually."

They both look at me, glance at each other, then back at me.

"We got time," Blake says.

I sigh deeply and try to figure out how exactly to phrase this without making myself sound completely and totally insane.

Maybe I should sound that way. Because maybe I am.

"Okay, well, when I first moved in, I decided to hire a cleaning service, like a housekeeping company, to come to the house a couple times a week."

"Sure. Naturally."

"As one does."

"Right, so after a quick Google search, I found this little business called Maid In Miami, where they specialize in cleaning high quality places and fancy homes and businesses. Perfect, right? So I scheduled a consultation with one of the owners."

"The rich guy and the maid," Blake says teasingly. "It's a tale as old as time."

"Well, she's not exactly the maid, she runs the company. And, well, she doesn't know that I'm...the rich guy."

Their blank stares prompt me to continue.

"I'll get to that. So, she shows up to the house for this consultation meeting, and I had honestly completely forgotten about it. I was pissed off at this stupid sprinkler in the front yard that wasn't working right, so I'd gone out to fix it. Which is what I was doing when she got there."

"And..." Blake narrows his gaze, clearly trying to understand where on earth this could possibly be going.

"And she thought I was...the gardener."

"Hah!" Dominic blurts out. "That's gold."

"Aw." Blake cocks his head. "That's weirdly kind of endearing."

Hope zings through me and I scoot forward, pointing at him enthusiastically. Maybe I'm not completely insane for feeling that way. "That's what I thought! It was...I don't know. Sweet. Amusing. And she's a total knockout from head to toe. With a dynamite personality as the cherry on top."

"Poor chick." Dominic shakes his head. "How embarrassed was she when you told her who you really are?"

"Oh, yeah..." Blake cringes and chuckles softly. "She must have been mortified."

"She, uh..." I scratch the back of my head, glancing off and sucking in a breath as I try and figure out how to explain this without sounding like an absolute psycho. "She didn't react."

They both look at me from across the table, waiting for me to continue.

"Because...I didn't tell her."

Silence falls over us as Blake and Dominic process what I've just said with some seriously confused expressions.

"You didn't...tell her?" Dominic repeats, drawing out the words.

"Wait, wait, wait..." Blake holds up a hand, shutting his eyes. "You didn't correct her? You just let her go on believing you were the gardener?"

"Well...yeah, kind of." I laugh dryly and run a hand through my hair. "It was a weird impulse decision to just sort of roll with it. It felt right in the moment and I...didn't correct her."

"Ever?" Blake asks, exasperated. "Like, at all?"

I let out a breath. "At all."

"She *still* thinks you're the gardener?" Dominic's jaw falls with shock and a laugh. "Hasn't she been back to the house to clean since then?"

I bite my lip. "Yeah."

Blake glares at me. "And...you're still pretending to be..."

"Yeah." I cut him off, cringing a little. "Look, I know it sounds...odd."

"Odd?" Dominic asks, drawing back. "Try absolutely, certifiably nuts is how it sounds."

Blake shakes his head, searching my face. "Dude. So now you're, like, keeping up this charade? You're still going with it? Every time she comes to the house to work you're going to have her believing you're the...gardener?"

"I...I don't know," I admit, my mind racing. "This isn't exactly something I planned on doing or gave a lot of thought to. It just...happened."

"What was going through your mind?" Blake laughs, swirling his beer around, completely riveted by my story.

"I couldn't tell you. Like I said, it wasn't a well-thought-out decision. It was just...she thought I was the gardener, and I never told her that I...wasn't."

"But you're into this girl?" Dominic asks, leaning forward and narrowing his gaze.

"Yeah, I mean..." I shrug. "Yeah, I am."

"And you think having her believe that you're a gardener instead of a hedge fund manager is a...*good* idea?"

"Seriously, bro," Blake chimes in. "If you want to get the girl, mentioning the whole billionaire thing seems more like a positive asset to me."

"No kidding," Dom snorts sarcastically.

"That's the thing guys. That's just it." I point my finger, gathering my thoughts. "The fact that she *doesn't* know who I am...she doesn't know about the money or the status or the job...it gives me this weird sense of...freedom. Like, there are no expectations or assumptions or..." I swallow and lower my gaze. "Ulterior motives."

They both stare back at me blankly, clearly not understanding why any guy in his right mind would omit the fact that he's loaded when trying to get a girl.

"It was kind of, I don't know, refreshing. In a way." I sip my beer.

"To fake being a gardener?" Dominic asks under his breath.

"To have a woman see me for more than just money," I explain. "I feel like, with Lilly, I can be whoever I want. I don't have to be Theodore the insanely wealthy investor. I can just be TJ. And if she likes me, she likes me for TJ. Not for my bank account."

"Because she doesn't know your bank account has nine zeroes in it," Blake clarifies slowly, studying me.

"Exactly."

"And you're saying," Dominic starts, "that her not knowing that is a *good* thing?"

"Look, I know it sounds bizarre."

"Yeah, slightly," Blake scoffs.

"And, again, it's not something I planned out or calculated or did on purpose. I just...didn't correct her."

"And now you're going on a date as..."

"The gardener."

The two of them laugh and shake their heads, taking this all in.

"I'm just confused." Blake ruffles his dark hair. "If you tell her the truth, she'll be head over heels for you. It makes you, like, a thousand times more attractive."

"But that's just it," I answer. "She'll fall for the wrong reasons. Look, it's just a stupid little escape. It's just something that I've gotten a bit carried away with. I'm just gonna have a little fun while I'm here in Florida for the winter. It's never going to be serious. You guys both know what happened to my dad, getting burned by my mom who only wanted him for the money and ran off with half of it."

I think back to my parents' acrimonious divorce, and my mom ditching him—and me, an only child—with a huge wad of cash to go be with the guy she'd been having an affair with. It always stuck with me as an example of just mercilessly using other people simply because they have money...faking love, faking family. I never want to experience that, and I'd gotten a small taste of it from some girls I dated casually at Cornell.

"Yeah..." Blake blows out a breath. "We remember. And that's completely brutal. But...hiding your real identity from someone?"

"It's a little sketchy, bro," Dom says softly.

"I know, I know. Like I said, I don't think it's gonna be anything serious or anything...at all. I just need to know what it's like. I'm rolling with it. For now. The other thing is that she made a comment to me, in passing. When we were at my house and she was there with her cleaning crew, she said something about how she can't stand super-rich types who get their money handed to them. She's all about self-made, hard work, starting from the bottom sort of thing."

Blake scoffs. "You didn't exactly start from the bottom, Teej."

"Yeah, no kidding. So now, not only will her entire perception of me change if and when she finds out the truth, but she also will automatically hate me. Not just for lying, but for being the exact thing she despises."

"This could seriously, majorly blow up in your face." Blake levels his eyes with mine. "You do know that, right?"

I finish off my beer with one last swig and lean my elbows onto the brown wooden table. "Yeah. I know."

"Well, you've officially made our lives look boring and mundane, so let's get another round and toast to living vicariously through TJ's terrible impulsive decisions."

I laugh and roll my eyes, wondering what in the world I've gotten myself into and how I could possibly get out.

They're right. This definitely could blow up in my face. But, who cares? I'm only here for the winter, as an escape. A hiatus from New York. I can have a little fun.

SEVEN

LILLY

"ARE YOU SURE THIS ISN'T TOO MUCH CLEAVAGE?" I angle my phone camera in front of my chest, with Bianca and Meredith on a FaceTime call.

"Yes," Bianca says with certainty.

"I don't know, Lil. It's definitely a bit...boobalicious," Meredith adds.

"Oh, Mer." Bianca clicks her tongue. "She's a hot single woman in Miami, not a nun. The top is perfect, Lilly."

I laugh nervously and adjust the V-neck of the black tank top I've paired with faded, ripped jeans and wedge sandals for my date with TJ. "Thanks, guys. I'm anxious."

"Don't be!" Bianca urges. "Have fun, relax, enjoy the free food."

Meredith laughs softly. "Just be yourself, Lilly. You already know this guy is crazy about you. If anything, he should be the one who's pacing around nervously."

"Am I pacing?" I ask, realizing that I've been constantly in motion for the last thirty minutes. "I didn't notice."

"You got this, chica." Bianca grins widely and gives me a big thumbs up through the phone screen.

"And we better get all the deets as soon as you're home," Meredith insists.

"Of course," I say, letting out a deep breath. "I'll call all four of you and share. Hopefully no horror stories, especially considering I have to see this guy at least two times a week if we want to keep Moneybags as a client."

"Does he work every day at that house?" Meredith asks. "There must be a lot of gardening to do..."

A knock on the door of my condo startles me, and I bring the phone right up to my face, keeping my voice hushed. "He's here! I have to go!"

"Love you, Lil!"

"Stay safe!"

"Bye!" I quickly hang up and take one last glance in the mirror I have hanging by the front door, happy I decided to keep my hair down. It's shiny and looking particularly voluminous. Thank you, hair gods.

I swing open my front door, drawing back as I come face to face with a man who somehow gets progressively hotter every time I lay eyes on him.

"Hi." I smile, tilting my chin up to meet his gaze, a substantial several inches above mine.

"Hey there." His voice is low, sexy enough to send a quick chill zipping through me. A soft smile pulls at his lips as his gaze slides over my body. "You look amazing."

"Thanks." I grab my purse and keys as I step out of my condo, shutting the door behind me. "You, uh, you clean up pretty nicely yourself," I say, in what is likely the biggest understatement of the century.

Of course, sweaty, dirty, outside TJ is insanely hot. But...freshly showered, tight white T-shirt and khaki pants with a hint of cologne TJ...now that really gets the butterflies going.

"So...did you pick a restaurant?" I ask, referring to the texts we'd exchanged this morning where he insisted on surprising me with a dinner spot.

"Actually, yes I did. And I think you're gonna love it."

Excitement zings through me as we walk across the parking lot of my building. I follow him as we head past several rows of cars.

"Where's your car?" I ask with a soft laugh, looking up at him as a salty breeze lifts my hair around my face.

"We're not taking my car." He slides my hand into his and guides me down the street. "We're walking."

"Walking, huh?" Maybe I should have gone with the flats. "What restaurants are that close to here?"

"I'm sorry, do you actually know what the word 'surprise' means?" he teases me, nudging my arm playfully.

I take it as an opportunity to feel the solid rock of his muscles against me, attraction making me giddy.

"Okay, okay." I wave my unoccupied hand. "Surprise."

We walk down a short, residential backroad that I know is the quickest way to the beach from my condo. The weather is absolutely perfect, warm without being crazy hot, the air breezy and clear and comfortable.

It's just about sunset, and the sky is a soft, faded orange with a few puffy clouds.

"I figured we'd be going downtown somewhere, but...I

can roll with a walk." I glance around, knowing we're still heading toward the beach. "But, I really don't think there're any restaurants down here. It's all residential and the beach area is more—"

"Seriously?" He flicks his brows, those deep brown eyes grabbing me.

"Right. Sorry." I bite my lip as we both laugh and keep walking through the salty ocean air.

"So we *are* going to the beach..." I clarify, wagging a finger at him as we reach a tiny, hidden beach access surrounded by palm trees and sea grapes.

"Nicely done, Sherlock." He winks as he guides me to the small, lush path and the sound of the ocean waves becomes louder and clearer with every step.

I slide him a look and follow him down the path, admiring his gorgeously cut back muscles and the strong confidence he walks with.

"Wow! The beach!" I exclaim jokingly. "I never thought we'd end up here."

He rolls his eyes and walks along the small boardwalk, leading to a set of stairs that goes down to the sand. "Just follow me."

"I'm telling you, we are not near any restaurants or places that would have—"

Before I can finish my sentence, I reach the end of the boardwalk and stand at the top of the staircase, my heart flipping at the sight in front of me.

A picnic. No—a fancy, detailed, extravagant-looking dinner for two. Sitting in the sand, there's a table set with a white tablecloth and flowers, dishes, glasses, even a candle. In the middle of the table, there's a beautiful white basket, decorated with more flower petals and a bottle of wine sticking out the top of it.

Two chairs sit on either side of the dinner setting, and there's literally no one around. It's private and intimate and *insanely* romantic.

"Holy crap..." I say through a laugh, bringing my hand to my mouth in shock as I stand at the top of the wooden staircase and stare at the scene in front of me, which looks like the cover of a fiction novel.

"See...I never actually used the word *restaurant*." TJ juts his chin at me and reaches his hand out to help me down the steps.

"This is seriously amazing. You...did this all for me?" I look up at him, his brown hair rippling in the sea breeze.

"No, I'm actually expecting someone else." He rolls his eyes and chuckles. "Yes, for you. Obviously."

I slide my feet out of my wedges and walk barefoot toward the picturesque dinner table, dropping my shoes into the sand as TJ pulls my chair out and I sit down.

"You like it?" he asks eagerly, his eyes bright and wide and painfully endearing.

"I...I love it." I shake my head, noting every thoughtful detail of the setup. "This is amazing. I mean, no one's ever done anything like this for me. Especially not for a first date."

"Well..." He lifts a shoulder. "I wanted it to be special. I know we don't know each other very well yet, but...I just thought it would be fun."

"I'm having a blast already."

We break into the picnic basket, pouring glasses of wine and setting up the different components of a charcuterie board that are all individually packaged inside the basket.

"You like cheese?" he asks me.

"Am I human? What kind of question is that?"

He tosses me a little container of mozzarella cubes and I laugh as I snatch it out of the air.

"I didn't know if you were, like, a vegan or something."

I pop a piece of mozz into my mouth, feeling weirdly comfortable and at ease. "I was a pescatarian for a year in college, if that counts."

TJ flicks his brows. "Impressive."

"Not really."

"So...college." He sips his wine and studies me, the genuine interest in my very existence making my heart flutter. "I take it you studied business?"

"Marketing, actually. In undergrad. Then I stayed for business school and got my MBA."

"All at UF?"

"Yup." I straighten my shoulders proudly. "Double Gator here."

He cuts some pepperoni slices and lays them out on the tray between us, glancing at me with a smile. "Well, go Gators, then."

"Absolutely." I tip my glass toward him and take a sip of what tastes like...wow. Expensive wine. "What about you? Have you always worked in gardening? Family business...?"

His eyes flash for a second and he glances away, making me wonder if maybe I shouldn't have asked that? I can't imagine why not, though...

"Uh, yeah. I do what my father does." He smiles, and I ignore the split second of weirdness a moment ago.

"Aw, that's sweet. Did he teach you everything you know?"

"Absolutely. He's definitely my mentor, and he works hard as can be." TJ reaches for the wine bottle and refills both of our glasses. "But I want to hear more about you. You started your own business with your best friends and now you're absolutely killing it. I mean, that's pretty impressive."

I sip the wine and feel myself blush. "Thank you. I'm just so lucky to be a business owner and to get to share everything with my girls. It's been an adventure for sure, but I know the best is still yet to come."

"Well, cheers to that." He raises his glass and shoots me a flirty look.

"Cheers." I tap mine to his, and notice a beautiful, shiny watch glimmering on his wrist. As he turns his arm, I get a look at the watch face. It's a Rolex.

I nod toward his wrist and chuckle. "Dang, ole Theodore must be paying you a killing," I tease.

"Oh." He waves a dismissive hand and quickly brings the watch down to his lap. "It was a gift, from my dad."

"Aw." I smile. "That's sweet."

"Where's your family? Do they live here?"

I push my hair behind my ears and bask in the warm enjoyment of talking to him. "Well, I grew up here, but when I went to college they moved up to Ponte Vedra, a bit south of Jacksonville. But Miami still feels like home, which is why we all decided to come back here after business school."

"That makes sense. It's a beautiful city, there's really no other place quite like it..."

"There really isn't."

We chat and talk and laugh as the sun goes down and evening fades into night. The weather stays flawless and the air feels dreamy. My head and heart are floaty and light, feeling like I could just lift off the ground and fly away.

I can't remember the last time I connected with a guy like this. Actually, I can. It was Aaron. But no one since him, not until tonight.

And now, somehow, the bottle of wine is empty, the food is finished, the sun is set, and I don't think either of us have stopped smiling since we sat down.

"Wait, okay, hold on..." TJ says through a laugh, holding up a hand. "You told me you started your business from a final project. You didn't mention it was a drunk five AM decision."

I tip my head back with laughter. "It kinda was. We had been up all night crushing bottles of champagne."

"Hey, graduation night."

"Exactly. And it just sort of happened."

"You know, most people, when they have a crazy idea at five in the morning after slamming champagne all night, just laugh about it the next day." He studies me, smiling with a twinkle in his eye that makes me feel seen and adored.

"We are not most people." I wag my finger. "When sobriety hit, the idea sounded even better."

We both laugh, and I let myself sit with the pure happiness of the night. TJ seems to be wildly fascinated with me, always asking question after question and genuinely listening to and caring about my answers.

But he doesn't talk much about himself. Which is refreshing, but I also am dying to know more.

"Should we pack it up? It's about to be completely dark out here, and I don't think this measly little candle is gonna be of much help to us." TJ taps the glass container of the candle that's melted away with the evening.

I let out a satisfied sigh and turn my face toward the salty ocean breeze. "Yeah, I suppose we should head back. But this was"—I lock my eyes with his, my heart picking up as he meets my gaze—"absolutely amazing. I had such a great night with you."

"I can't remember having this much fun on a date... ever," he says, his expression sparking with sincerity.

I laugh softly and let warmth fill my chest as we pack everything up.

"I'll, um..." He gestures back at the table. "I'll take care of all this."

"Oh, please. I don't mind helping." I wave a hand. "I clean up for a living, remember? Well, sort of."

"Seriously, it's fine." TJ steps closer to me, the moonlight glinting in his gaze. I can smell that sexy cologne again and butterflies soar through me. "Wanna take a little walk?"

Excitement flutters at the prospect of this night not coming to an end just yet. "Sure."

EIGHT

TJ

TECHNICALLY, I HAVEN'T TOLD A LIE. NOT ONE SINGLE lie. I do, in fact, work the same job as my father. And the Rolex, thank God, was actually a gift from him. In an effort to dodge certain questions, I've been steering the conversation almost entirely back to Lilly. Which has given me the chance to dive a bit deeper and start really getting to know her, so I really can't complain at all.

She loved my picnic-style dinner on the beach, which was a last minute plan that I came up with as I was getting ready for the date, and I realized that me pulling up in a $200,000 car might lead to some doubts about my identity.

I know, I know. It's a little schemy. And I'm pretty pissed at myself for it. But...I just can't let it go. I can't let go of the intoxicating freedom of dating a woman with absolutely *no* agenda. No plans, no motives. She just...likes me. It's so new and insanely liberating.

An escape is what I wanted, and that's exactly what I'm getting.

"So..." Lilly threads her fingers through mine as we walk barefoot along the shoreline in the dark, warm sand squishing between my toes. "I want to hear more about you! I feel like I've talked your ear off all night about my exceptionally uninteresting life."

"Okay, well, we both know that's not true." I nudge her softly.

Great. She wants to know more about me. I want to tell her all about myself and my life, I want to tell her everything. But I can't give this up...I can't ruin everything.

Especially considering the fact that she made her feelings on rich, trust fund types extremely clear. She'd hate the real me. She'd run away so far and fast from a hedge fund billionaire that I'd never see her again.

But not the gardener. She adores the gardener. And I feel more like myself with her than I have in years.

Yikes. Tangled web.

"Okay..." I swing our hands together between us as a wave gently splashes onto the shore. "What do you want to know?"

"Are you from Miami, too?"

"No, I'm from New York." I kick a shell. "My family is all up there, still."

"Like New York City?" she asks, turning to me with intrigue.

"Manhattan, yeah." I bite my lower lip. "Have you been?"

"A couple of times, when I was younger. It's a little cold up there for me; I'm a Florida girl." She gives an easy laugh and lifts a shoulder, somehow becoming more attractive by the second. "What brought you down here, then?"

"I just..." I let out a breath, once again making a concerted effort not to lie. "I needed a change. It is cold up there, in more ways than one. I wanted new scenery, new culture, new people. So, I just kinda sent it down here."

"Full send, I love that."

"Always full sends," I tease, bumping her side as we walk down the beach.

"You've got to have hobbies other than gardening, right? What else are you into? Now that you know my entire life story from dinner."

"I know that you've never dyed your hair and you're a huge Heat fan and you made the decision to start a business when you were drunk."

Lilly laughs, musical and bubbly. "You're a good listener."

"I try." I run a hand through my hair. "Hobbies, well...I like to work out."

"Really?" She fakes a gasp and draws back, her eyes wide and her smile bright as she looks directly at my biceps. "I *never* would have guessed."

"Ha ha," I say playfully. "I, uh, I also like to paint. Well, I used to." The words surprise me, considering I haven't told anyone about my childhood hobby in years.

"You paint?" She glances up at me, beaming. "That's awesome."

"Used to paint. I'm just so busy with work now, I hardly ever have the time to really sit down and do it. It's been ages since I've had a paintbrush in my hand, but I really miss it. There was something so calming about it, like your mind just shuts off all the worries and fears and stress and focuses on nothing but the brush and the canvas. But, I don't know. It's been a long time, feels like another lifetime that I was into that."

We both pause as Lilly listens and nods slowly.

"Anyway," I say quickly, waving a hand. "Just a silly thing."

"It's not silly," she says sternly. "It's awesome."

"Thanks." I smile, feeling weirdly...understood. "My mom was a big painter. She showed me how to do it when I was super little, and I loved it all growing up."

"Where is she now? In New York with your dad?"

"Uh...no." I clear my throat as our pace slows to a stop and I hold Lilly's comforting blue gaze. "She and my dad split when I was nine, and she just kinda...ran off. I guess there was another man and she left to be with that guy or... whatever." I shake off the story and omit the part about my dad being a billionaire and my mom taking a bunch of money.

"Oh, gosh." Lilly sighs sadly and holds her hand to her chest. "That must have been awful. You were at such a tender age."

"I survived." I give a half smile and try to lighten up the mood. "I got really close with my dad through it all, and that ended up being great. But I haven't picked up a paint-brush since she left."

What the heck am I doing? Just dumping my sob story onto this poor girl like she's my therapist? The truth and emotions and rawness of it just pours out of me with total ease, and it's honestly kinda freaky. This is stuff I don't talk about. Ever, to anyone. I usually push it away into the very back corners of my mind and go weeks without thinking of it.

And yet, here I am, on a date with a woman I basically just met, and I'm feeling the most relaxed and open and vulnerable that I can remember.

"Oh, wow," Lilly says softly after considering and processing my story. "I'm so sorry all of that happened to you."

"Please." I give a dry laugh. "It was forever ago. And everything turned out fine."

"You should start painting again!" she exclaims, enthusiasm radiant in her voice.

"Oh..." I shrug carelessly, hiding the fact that the very idea of that makes me tense. "I don't know. It was just a childhood activity. I doubt I'm even any good anymore."

"You don't have to be good at something to enjoy it."

I look at Lilly, reading her expression. "Well, yeah. That's true."

"Are you happy?" She tilts her chin up to lock eyes with me, the bluntness of the question catching me a little off guard.

"Right now? Yeah, extremely. I haven't connected with someone like this in—"

"No, I mean, like, with your life. In general. Are you happy?"

I shut my eyes and let out a breath, relaxing a little.

With her, as TJ the unassuming gardener who has picnics on the beach and talks about his past and attracts a woman like Lilly McCarthy? Yes. Yes, I'm very happy with that life.

Except it's not *my* life. It's an escape. Just like the house, just like Miami, just like the winter.

"Yeah." I nod, reaching out to tuck a strand of silky blonde hair behind her ears. "I'm happy. Especially now that I met you."

Her beautiful, delicate face flushes pink, and the glimmer in her eye lets me know that the feeling is mutual. Her hair falls in soft waves around her shoulders, and it's the first time I've seen her with it down. She's absolutely mesmerizing, balancing the blend between sexy and cute like I've never seen.

"What about you?" I ask softly, my voice husky and low as we stand along the shoreline, the waves just barely kissing our toes as they crash onto the sand.

"What *about* me?" Her lips lift into a smile, this one hot and flirty.

"Are you happy?"

She glances down then back up at me. "Yeah, I am. But something has been missing for a long time."

"I feel the same way."

"And..." She swallows, visibly letting her guard down. "I feel like I might have just found it."

Without another word, I take her face with both my hands and press my lips to hers, passion and chemistry rising in my chest. She tastes like sunshine and red wine, and with her mouth against mine, the entire world starts to fade away.

She kisses me back, sweet and gentle, but with some tangible desire. The breeze blows around us with a slight chill, and I move my arms around Lilly's waist, savoring the way she fits me as perfectly as a puzzle piece.

She lets out something like a laugh, smiling against my mouth as she runs her hand through my hair.

We kiss a little more, heat building like wildfire between us. I never want this moment to end. I never want this night to end. I know that it has to—and I have to face the confusing and tangled reality of my life.

But, man, I wish I could be TJ the Gardener forever. Because Lilly adores me, and I'm completely enamored with her. Almost as enamored as I am with the feeling of being separated from my money and status for once.

But...it's not real. It can't be. And that...freaking sucks.

NINE

LILLY

I'm still floating around on a cloud on Monday morning as I breeze into the office. For the first time in almost a year, I don't think about how small our shoebox of a workspace is. I don't think about how I wish we could get into a bigger, nicer office and not have to have our desks pushed up against each other. I don't even think about unanswered emails or phone calls or whatever cautionary numbers and risk factors Aubrey is inevitably going to tell me about.

I don't think about anything but how the sun is shining, the day is new, and holy cow...I like a guy. Like...a lot.

"Good morning, my beautiful besties," I sing as I walk over to sit down on my desk, my signature ponytail swinging behind me.

"There you are!" Cici looks up from her computer, her eyes wide.

"We want to hear *more!*" Meredith insists with a bright laugh.

"I FaceTimed all of you guys after the date and told you everything. I swear, I left out no details." I take a sip of my coffee. "What more do you need?"

Aubrey sighs dramatically, pushing her computer glasses up onto her forehead. "We just want to live vicariously through you. Again."

I snort and shake my head. "I swear, I told you everything. It was...a dream." I glance out the window at the subpar view, which looks more beautiful than ever today. "I haven't found the fatal flaw yet."

"Who says there has to be one?" Bianca asks loudly as she strolls into the office with a big, brown paper bag in her hand.

"Finally," Aubrey says with a laugh, rolling her eyes.

"I know, I know." Bianca waves her hand apologetically. "I'm late as usual. But...to make up for it, I brought donuts!" She wiggles the bag around and plops it down on her desk.

"And you are forgiven," Meredith says with a nod, digging into the bag.

"I'm doing no sugar, no carbs," Cici says, scrolling through something on her computer.

"Really, Ci?" I slide her a look. "You're as fit as an Instagram model. You live in the gym. You should eat whatever the heck you want. Life is short. And good. And happy."

"Wow, okay." Meredith laughs, drawing back and studying me. "This mood is especially cheery, even for you. And that's saying something."

"Friday night must have been one wild ride." Bianca shakes her shoulders and gives me a playful wink. "Huh?"

"We did not sleep together." I cross my arms and lean back in my desk chair. "We just kissed. A lot. And talked. And..." I draw in a slow breath. "Oh my gosh, you guys, I like him so much," I burst out through giddy laughter. "I feel like a ninth grader with a crush."

"Oh, my heart." Bianca holds her chest dramatically. "Too cute for words."

"We're so happy for you, Lil." Meredith smiles sweetly. "Seriously."

"We love you and want you to be happy," Aubrey adds. "Just be careful. I would really hate to see you get hurt."

"I know, I know. And I want to take it slow and ease into things and see where it goes. I just..." I raise my hands and lower them, centering myself. "Have a really good feeling. But, you're right, Aubs. I can't get too ahead of myself."

"You're a dreamer, Lilly." Cici lifts a shoulder and grins at me. "And this is so exciting."

"It really is." I force myself to focus on work and the exponentially growing business, so I open up my computer and start sifting through my tasks for the week.

"When do you see him again?" Cici asks.

"Well, we're cleaning the Rinehart guy's house tomorrow, so I'll go there to supervise and see him then. I'm not sure if he works every day or what, but I figure he'll be there."

"Rinehart guy..." Aubrey taps a pen against her lips and furrows her brow, looking up at me from behind her laptop. "Have you still not met him? The owner of the house?"

I shake my head slowly, pursing my lips. "I have not. He's seriously elusive."

"Really?" Meredith asks, surprised.

"I mean..." Aubrey looks back down at her computer screen, narrowing her gaze to read something closely. "He's an official client. We've already received an electronic payment from him, and everything is signed and cleared."

"So, we know he exists," Bianca says, taking a bite of a donut with pink frosting and sprinkles, "and is in communication with us...sort of."

"Of course he exists," I say on a dry laugh. "I've been to his house."

"And he's..." Aubrey wrinkles her nose, skeptical. "Never there? He just lets you and the team come in, clean, and leave without any kind of contact?"

"It is pretty weird, I'll admit," Meredith adds, breaking up a chocolate glazed.

"Yeah..." I shrug and turn back and forth in my chair. "I suppose it's a little weird, but, hey. You've got to work quite a lot to make a billion dollars, so I'm sure his cleaning staff is just about the last thing on his mind."

Bianca sips her coffee and flicks a hand. "You're definitely right, Lil. No need to question the deepest pockets we've ever cleaned for, right?"

"Fair enough." Cici waves a finger.

"Oh, wow." Aubrey blurts out suddenly, her eyes wide with shock as she stares at something on her computer screen.

"What?" Cici stands up and jogs around the desk to see.

"What is it?" I ask, worry rising in my chest.

"Apparently..." Aubrey narrows her gaze as we all flock around her desk and study the computer screen. "Zachary Thorne is building a mansion in Miami Beach. Evidently."

"Zachary Thorne?" I exclaim, gasping with the news. "You mean *the* Zachary Thorne...as in one of the biggest rock stars in the business?

"Holy cow, you guys." Cici bounces on her toes. "This is huge."

"We have got to get his business. Our first *real*, big name, A-list celebrity...and it's falling right in our laps!" Aubrey clasps her hands together with cautious excitement.

"This is such an opportunity," Bianca says with a grin, flipping her hair over her shoulder and leaning forward to scan the article on the computer once more. "Good lord, he's cute."

"Insanely cute," Cici agrees.

"The guy's definitely a looker," I chime in, glancing at the photo of Zachary Thorne, who's giving a smoldering look to the camera, his blue eyes stunningly sexy. Shaggy blond hair falls carelessly around his sharp, chiseled face. He has a guitar slung over his back and his entire image oozes *bad boy*.

"We're gonna fight over the supervisor position for *that* client, that's for sure," Bianca jokes.

"Oh, no. You can count me out." Meredith, who's been quiet for this whole conversation, steps back and waves her hand. "I'm all for the big business for our company, but I want nothing to do with that guy."

"Oh, Mer." Bianca rolls her eyes and gives an easy smile. "He's a rock star. He doesn't bite."

"Who knows? He might," Aubrey teases with a chuckle.

Meredith just shakes her head insistently. "No way. He's got...tattoos. And a reputation. We've all read the articles about him. He's a total bad boy. He's probably going to be having wild, debauchery-filled parties at that mansion every night of the week, with people doing God knows what." She cringes and winkles her nose. "It scares me."

"Sounds to me like it'll be getting really, really *messy*..." Bianca winks. "And he's going to need a lot of cleaning."

"I'm making a note to get in contact with his representatives shortly before he moves here, assuming these rumors are true. Nothing is official yet, but if it is..." Aubrey types furiously on her keyboard. "We'll secure his business."

"Hey," I wave a hand and laugh. "I'll personally go in there and pick up a thousand sticky red Solo cups every day if it means Maid In Miami has a celebrity client."

"True that," Cici agrees. "I'm so hyped! We're going to be huge, you guys...I can feel it." She flips her long, black ponytail and flops back into her desk chair. "Fingers crossed our next celeb is a professional athlete who can sweep me off my feet and carry me away into the sunset on his massive shoulders..."

I laugh and shake my head. "Any and all athletes will automatically go to you, Ci. Promise."

She blows me a kiss and turns back to her computer.

Suddenly, Bianca gasps, looking at her phone.

"What is it? Another super famous rock star moving to Miami so we can pounce?" I ask enthusiastically.

"No. It's my mother," she answers, glancing up at me. "She and my aunt and three little cousins are coming to town for the weekend. I completely and totally forgot, and have absolutely nothing planned."

"There's always the beach," Meredith suggests.

"The Gardens?" Aubrey throws in.

"A South Florida Riders game? They play at home this weekend," Cici adds.

"I don't know..." Bianca shakes her head. "Dang, and I thought I was gonna have time to lay some major groundwork with Alec the Hot Bartender this weekend."

Aubrey rolls her eyes. "You've been laying groundwork with him for two years, B."

"He wants me," she insists with a laugh. "He just doesn't know it yet."

"I know!" Meredith exclaims. "You could take them to the zoo!"

Just the mention of the word "zoo" sends me into a spiral of happy nostalgia, my mind flashing with images of my absolute favorite childhood place. My dad worked there as a groundskeeper and cleaner, so we got in for free. My mom took me all the time growing up, and I never stopped loving it.

As my friends mull over ideas and chat, I lean back in my chair and feel my heart squeeze at the memories. Suddenly, I have to go to the zoo. I haven't been in way, way too long.

And I know exactly who I want to bring.

TEN

TJ

CRAP!

I see the bright pink Maid In Miami van pull into the driveway out of the corner of my eye and the women start unloading their equipment.

I glance down at myself. I had to shave and put on a nice button-down for a Zoom meeting this morning, and I'm freshly showered with combed hair.

She's gonna know. She's gonna realize that gardeners don't dress like this for work and she's gonna see me come out of the office and...it's all going to get completely destroyed.

My mind races for a quick second as I stand up from my desk, peeking out the window.

There's Lilly, sporting that typical, long ponytail and wearing black jeans and a MIM T-shirt. She's laughing about something with her crew members, throwing her head back and smiling at the sun.

God, she's radiant.

Okay, TJ. This is it. This is how she finds out, and there's absolutely no possible way I can talk my way out of this. I'm just gonna have to come clean, and deal with the consequences, and—

No. I can't. Not yet.

In a frantic and shamefully embarrassing moment, I yank off the button-down and shove it into my desk drawer, ruffle around my hair so it looks messy, and slip out of the office, locking it as quickly as I can before she and her team come to the front door.

I hear the knock a couple of seconds later, and glance down at myself. Sweatpants and no shirt...well, it's more believable than the button-down. I'll just have to go with it.

I swing open the front door, coming face to face with those enchanting, deep blue eyes. "Hey there."

"Hi." Lilly looks a little surprised to see me and glances over my shoulder. "Are you always, like, in charge around here?"

I run a hand through my hair. "I have a broad job description. Plus, I'm always here first thing in the morning. You know, for the..." I rack my brain. "Plants."

"Right." She narrows her gaze a little and gives a soft smile. "Is Theodore here, do you know?" She walks past me with the four other women in tow, stepping into the entryway and front living room, where warm sunlight is pouring in through the sliding glass doors. "I just would really like to meet him; it's crazy that I haven't."

"Ah, you just missed him," I say quickly, trying not to visibly wince at the lie.

"Dang." She wrinkles her nose. "He's a hard man to get in contact with."

"You have no idea," I mumble, glancing down at the floor. "Anyway, I better..." I point a finger out to the backyard. "Get back to work."

Her gaze lingers on mine for an extra beat, those sweet pink lips parting like she wants to say something but is too distracted by the moment to really think about what it is. Or maybe that's just how I'm feeling.

"Right," she finally whispers, her lips lifting into a slow smile. "I'm gonna head upstairs with the girls."

"Okay." I smile.

"Okay." Lilly draws out the word, letting the moment linger for an extra few seconds, the tension and attraction between us crackling like fire.

Her chest rises and falls as she keeps her eyes locked with mine and I *almost* kiss her again, but she turns around and walks toward the long, curved staircase. Her ponytail swings from side to side and I can't help but take a long look at her flawless and gorgeous body as she walks away.

Desire ripples through me as I shake my head and open the sliding glass door, walking out onto the back patio and pool deck.

What is actually wrong with me? I should have told her day one. I should have come clean. Now I'm in way, way too deep.

I just got so wrapped up in the liberating feeling of it all, not to mention the fact that she would absolutely hate the real me... Now I'm deep into this hot mess and I'm starting to catch feelings and I think Blake and Dominic were right: this very well could blow up in my face.

"Hey," Lilly's voice calls to me, bringing me out of my thoughts as I pace around the pool.

"Oh, hey." I squint into the sun to see her stepping out onto the deck and sliding the door closed behind her.

"This is...this is kind of weird and random, but..." She holds a hand up to shield her eyes from the sunlight as she walks around the pool to get closer to me. "Would you want to go to the zoo with me?"

"The zoo?" I laugh, drawing back in surprise.

"Yeah, Zoo Miami. It's, um...it's kind of special to me. I haven't been in forever and someone mentioned it the other day and..." She waves a hand. "You can totally say no."

"I would love to go to the zoo with you." The words tumble out with honesty and ease.

Her eyes light up, making my heart squeeze. "Really? Okay, cool! Saturday?"

"Saturday it is." I grin. "Oh, but would you mind driving? My car is..." *One of the six-figure sports cars in the garage.* "In the shop."

"Sure, no worries! I could get there in my sleep." She smiles over her shoulder as she starts to walk away.

I get the feeling that going to the zoo is going to open up even more pieces to the puzzle of Lilly McCarthy, and the idea is thrilling.

And I can keep opening up to her...carefully.

There's no good way to tell her. There's no possible way to tell her and still have a chance of even remotely being in her life.

I lean back and look at the house in all its glory. Money, money, money. Being seen for something other than this is a fantasy and an escape and the way I always knew dating should feel. And I just want to live in that fantasy a *little* bit longer.

ELEVEN

LILLY

"We're here." I grin widely, unable to contain the joy that warms my heart as I pull into the parking lot of Zoo Miami. "Are you ready to see some animals?" I turn to TJ in the passenger's seat, shaking his shoulders.

He laughs and smiles brightly. "Heck yes I am."

"Let's go!" I hop out of the car and lock it before walking around to his side and reaching for his hand. We've only hung out a few times, but somehow acting like a couple with TJ feels...natural. It feels right. And bringing him here feels like the next perfect date.

As we walk up to the familiar entrance, I turn to TJ, taking a long look at the gorgeous specimen of a man on my arm.

He's in khaki shorts and a light blue T-shirt that hugs his strong, masculine physique flawlessly. I notice that he shaved recently, and has just the slightest shadow darkening his jawline.

I opted for a pink sundress because, despite the fact that it's almost December, it's definitely toasty out.

"So...I have to know." He glances down at me, a flirty crooked smile playing on his lips. "Why is the zoo so special to you? You a big animal girl?"

"I mean, don't get me wrong, I love animals. I have three cats."

He laughs and draws back. "Oh man. Don't tell me I'm dating a crazy cat lady."

I giggle and shake my head. "I don't trust anyone who doesn't like cats. You have to *earn* their love and affection. You have to work for it."

I can see his playfully narrowed gaze even through the lenses of his sunglasses. "Why would I want to have to convince my *pet* to love me?"

"Not love." I hold up a finger. "Tolerate."

"I'm a dog person." He lifts a shoulder. "I'm all about that unconditional love."

I laugh and roll my eyes. "Well, to answer your original question, yes. I am a huge animal person. But that's not the only reason I love the zoo."

"Well..." He cocks his head. "What's the other?"

Right after he asks the question, we reach the front of the line to buy our tickets, and I instantly recognize two familiar, friendly faces behind the counter.

"Linda! Betty!" I wave and bounce on my toes, smiling at two of the many members of the zoo staff that felt like family to me growing up.

"Sweet heavens, Lilly McCarthy is that you?" Linda moves a long, gray braid over her shoulder and pushes her glasses up to study me closely. "Betty!" She gets the attention of the woman next to her.

I just smile and glance over at TJ, who is confused and intrigued.

"Good lord." Betty holds her hand to her heart dramatically. "Is that Billy McCarthy's girl? No. It can't be!"

I give a soft laugh and hold up my hand. "It is. How are you guys? It's been so long!"

"You're all grown up and..." Linda shakes her head in disbelief. "And absolutely beautiful. My goodness! How is your father, dear? And your mom?" She turns to TJ with absolutely no introduction, just talking to him as if he's part of the crew. "Oh, I adored this sweet little girl and her family."

I laugh and gesture toward him. "This is TJ, by the way."

"Boyfriend? Husband?" Betty demands, looking him up and down.

"Uh, just..." I share a look with him and bite back an awkward laugh. "A friend."

They glance at each other and communicate with some sort of telepathy.

"Well, my dear." Linda levels her gaze with me. "You and your 'friend' here are in for a treat. The new and improved meerkat exhibit just opened last week, and those little buggers are out and about."

"Social creatures," Betty adds with an affirming nod. "They sure are."

I look at TJ, who's just smiling and trying to process why on earth I would be so close with the ticket counter workers at the zoo. "I'm down for some meerkats," he says enthusiastically.

"Thank you, both." I smile sweetly at Linda and Betty. "It was wonderful to see you guys."

"Give your parents our best!" Betty calls as we take our tickets and head through the gate.

"I will!"

We take a few steps into the zoo, which is bustling with families and kids and couples looking at maps, taking pictures, or eating ice cream.

I take a deep breath and let the warm nostalgia wash over me.

"Okay..." TJ turns to me and crosses his arms. "I have got to know what's happening here." He laughs and looks back in the direction of the ticket counter.

"Okay, okay." I take his hand as we start walking down the main path of the zoo. "My dad used to work here, pretty much my whole childhood."

"He was in management?"

"Uh, no. He was more like a...groundskeeper. Kind of like what you do, but way, *way* less glamorous. You don't spend too much of your time cleaning elephant poop at the Rinehart house, I'd imagine."

"So you came here a lot?"

I smile at the memories as we walk past a pond filled with pink flamingos. "Like, every single weekend. We got in for free, obviously, so this was pretty much where I spent the vast majority of my free time. I used to sit at a picnic table and do my homework while I waited for my dad to get done working. Sometimes, he'd take me back to see animals and let me feed them. It was amazing. This zoo was like my second home and, as you can tell, the staff was like my second family."

TJ looks at me, his smile growing as admiration glimmers in his eyes. "Well, thanks for bringing me. It's really nice to get to know you more in a place that means so much to you."

I lift a shoulder and adjust my sunglasses. "I thought so, too. So...where to first?"

"You're the zoo expert." He gestures forward. "Guide us, Steve Irwin."

I tilt my head back and laugh, the warmth of the sunshine matching the warmth in my heart. "All right, let's start with the Amazon Jungle, and we can just make a big loop around the whole zoo."

"I'm game." He effortlessly reaches down for my hand, lacing his strong, masculine fingers through mine and giving me a slight squeeze.

Butterflies tickle my chest as we march forward into an unforgettable day.

"That's like you." TJ points to a brightly colored tropical bird that's hopping around in a tree.

"How is that like me?" I laugh softly, angling my head.

"She's blonde..."

"More like golden, but okay."

"Well, you're golden. And she's got all kinds of energy. Just bopping around, making everyone smile." He nudges me. "Like you. That's your spirit animal."

"A blue and yellow macaw, huh?" I flip my hair over my shoulder and keep my other hand glued to his. "I'll keep that in mind. Now we've gotta find your spirit animal."

As we wander slowly through the loops of Zoo Miami,

stopping to admire every exhibit and study the beautiful, majestic animals, time seems to melt away and everything feels light and breezy.

The sun is warm and the conversation is fun and easy and happy, and I can't stop thinking about how glad I am that I brought him here. I know it's early...I know it's way too soon...but I can't help but think that there could be something really special between us.

I don't want to get my hopes up, but...oops. I think they're already in outer space.

"Chicken tenders and fries at the zoo," I sing as we sit down at the outdoor café wielding baskets of steamy chicken strips. "Is there anything better?"

"There truly can't be." TJ holds up a fry and gazes at it lovingly. "This is peak happiness, right here."

I squeeze some ketchup onto a napkin and laugh softly, sliding into the shaded area of our picnic table. "I couldn't agree more."

"So, is this where you would do your homework as a kid?" he asks, sipping a cup of Diet Coke.

"Yeah," I say, smiling at the thought. "Yeah, I'd set up right at these tables with a little bowl of soft serve chocolate ice cream and crank out my math homework."

"It's the little things." TJ grins.

"It definitely was for me, that's for sure." A soft breeze blows the hair around my face, and I catch his gaze...deep and sincere and comforting. I feel a sudden desire to tell him more. To tell him everything. And why fight it? He's awesome. "Growing up, the zoo was, like, all I had."

TJ nods slowly, listening and waiting for me to continue.

I pop a fry into my mouth and shrug. "We didn't have much money, as you can imagine. My dad worked here and my mom bounced around a bunch of different retail jobs, but none of them lasted very long. I came from very, very little. It wasn't always fun growing up poor, but I always had so much love around me. It made it okay."

"Wow." TJ shakes his head, reaching across the table to gently touch my hand. "You've come a dang long way, Lilly."

I smile with pride. "I have. And it definitely wasn't always easy for me. Especially being in Miami...sometimes it really feels like a city of have's and have nots. And the have's..." I laugh dryly, widening my eyes. "Boy, do they *have*."

His eyes flash for a second and he glances away, making me wonder if something about that bothered him.

"Anyway," I continue, "I just grew to really value hard work and commitment. As cheesy as it sounds, my dad always told me I could do anything I put my mind to, even though I came from absolutely nothing. Hard work beats anything else, you know? Including"—I roll my eyes—"trust funds and foreign bank accounts and all the ritzy glitzy entitled finance jerks scattered across this city."

TJ chuckles a little, running a hand through his hair. "There sure are a lot of those around here."

"Ivy League dudes who were born into connections and zillion-dollar handouts. And I'm pretty sure we both work for one, considering I still haven't even freaking *met* the guy. Can you believe that?"

"No that's..." He wipes the corner of his mouth with a brown paper napkin. "That's pretty crazy. But he's super busy, especially in the mornings when you and your crew come."

"I get that." I finish off my last fry. "It just seems weird, to be getting a paycheck from someone I've never even had an in-person conversation with."

"I wouldn't sweat it too much," TJ says quickly, glancing down at a friendly pigeon hopping around underneath our table. "As long as you're getting paid, right?"

I shrug. "Yeah, I guess. I normally like to have personal relationships with my clients, but, hey. Maybe considering the soap box I just got down from, it's better if I never meet him," I say jokingly.

"I think that's very possible," TJ says, something in his tone suddenly shifting to a more serious note. "Can I give this guy a fry?" He nods down toward the bird.

"He's expecting it," I say with a soft laugh.

"Talk about entitled." TJ shoots me a wink that makes my heart kick a little. "Here, buddy." He flicks a piece of a fry onto the ground, and the pigeon promptly gobbles it up and stares at him, waiting for more. "Maybe this is my spirit animal."

"The entitled pigeon?" I laugh heartily and shake my head. "I think you're about the furthest thing from entitled."

TJ swallows, his gaze flashing a little. "Wanna keep going?"

"Yes, definitely." I stand up and smooth out the skirt of my dress. "Sorry, I just got to rambling there. I feel so weirdly comfortable around you, like I just wanna tell you everything about—"

"Hey." He stands up, leveling his gaze with mine. His

voice is low and controlled, giving me a chill as he steps closer with a cool smile. "Please don't apologize. You're endlessly fascinating, and I could listen to you for hours." He brushes by me to toss the trash in a receptacle and glances over his shoulder. "And, for what it's worth, I feel the same way. The whole...weirdly comfortable thing."

I smile at this, reaching over naturally to take his hand in mine again. "Then tell me more about you! Please."

He waves a dismissive hand as we start heading down the main path. "I'm not even remotely interesting compared to you."

"I highly doubt that."

"Well, it's true. Now, come on. I want to see some elephants."

I glance behind us to see the hungry, entitled pigeon hopping along the path, following us as we walk.

"Look," I nod toward the bird, laughing.

"Oh, wow." TJ chuckles and smiles down at the ground. "I've got myself a friend."

"He really likes you."

"He thinks I might be hiding more fries in my back pocket." He shakes his head, and the bird keeps hopping along in step with the two of us.

"He adores you. Look at those eyes."

"Maybe he does adore me." TJ holds his hand to his heart dramatically and laughs. "He can't seem to take his eyes off of me, can he?"

"I think..." I look to the side and up at TJ, looping my arm through his and feeling his strong, solid body against me. "I think that makes him *my* spirit animal."

TWELVE

TJ

"I HAD SUCH AN AWESOME DAY." I SMILE AT LILLY AS I hold the door open to Ben's—a small, slightly upscale cocktail bar without a lot of pretense in South Beach—where we decided to go get some drinks and hang out after our little zoo adventure.

"Oh my gosh," she says on a contented sigh as we step inside, the air conditioning blasting us both with a cool chill. "I had so much fun. It was great to be back."

"You said you hadn't been back in years, right?" I ask, guiding us over to a corner booth. The room is dimly lit, with soft music playing in the background and people quietly sipping drinks and chatting and keeping to themselves.

"Yes, it's been forever." Lilly slides into the booth. "I just got so caught up with the business after graduation, I hadn't had time to make it back. I'm really glad we went; that was a blast."

I smile and shake my head. "I haven't done something for the pure sake of fun like that in...as long as I can remember."

"Well, you deserve to have fun." She reaches across the table and takes my hand, her smile beaming. "You should paint again. I bet that would be fun."

"Psh." I force a laugh and wave off the comment, bothered by the very idea of spending time doing something so artsy and unproductive and...tied to my mom. "I doubt I could even make anything look halfway decent."

"You could always do, like, modern art." She laughs softly and lifts a slender shoulder, her blonde hair bouncing around her face. "You know, just a bunch of colors and patterns and paint splatters. Some of those sell for millions, and it doesn't even have to be a picture of anything."

"You are quite the optimist, aren't you?" I give a teasing wink, enjoying every second spent getting to know her.

She raises her brows, her blue eyes glimmering in the soft light. "What was your first clue?"

I order us drinks and we sip and laugh and relax, every moment feeling even easier and more natural than the one before. As I lose myself in conversation and chemistry and attraction, I try to push away the nagging voice in the back of mind that's cursing me for living a lie.

I have a pretty strong feeling that my window of time where it would have been even remotely acceptable to tell her the truth has totally sealed shut. If I tell her now, I'll look like a phony. An actor. A *liar*.

The thought stabs my gut and I try to shake it off and force a smile as I listen to Lilly tell me about how she met her best friends in business school.

I haven't told her I went to Cornell. I haven't told her... anything. And yet, I feel like she knows me better than anyone I've dated in years.

How is that possible? And how can I ever even begin to untangle this holy hot mess of a web?

I can't. There's no answer. There's no solution. As soon as my little winter escape is over, I can go back to New York. That's about the best answer there is and...wow, does it suck.

It sucks almost as much as knowing that Lilly would absolutely despise the real me. If she knew I was Theodore Rinehart Junior and I manage a completely different kind of *hedge* than the ones in the backyard.

What was supposed to be a fun fling as part of my Manhattan Hiatus has started to get really deep really fast, and the more time I spend lost in those blue eyes and enchanted by that sparkling personality, the deeper these feelings get. And the worse the situation gets.

Despite the fact that I've somehow unintentionally slipped into maintaining a false identity, I've had the most incredible time with her, and everything in me wishes it didn't have to end.

"So, that's Cici for you," Lilly continues on about her friends, smiling with pride when she talks about everyone close to her. "She's our token gym rat and absolute sports freak."

"Does she go to South Florida Riders games a lot?" I ask.

"Are you kidding?" Lilly snorts. "She's got season tickets."

"Figures." I smile and swirl my drink. "So you've got

Cici the sporty girl, Bianca the wild one, Aubrey who loves pro and con lists..."

"Emphasis on the cons." Lilly raises her finger with a soft laugh. "She's our risk manager."

"Got it. And then Meredith, who's the shy and innocent one."

"Yeah, we call her Virgin Mer."

"That's hilarious," I say on a laugh. "And then there's... Lilly the Leader." I beam at her, and her face flushes the slightest shade of rosy pink.

"Oh"—she flicks her hand—"I don't know about leader..."

"You are a leader," I say. "You came up with the whole idea for Maid In Miami."

"Well"—Lilly twists a strand of her hair—"I suppose I did, technically."

"Your friends all sound awesome." I sip my beer. "I'd love to meet them." The words come flying off my tongue so naturally and easily, I forget to stop and think that the very *last* thing I should be doing is getting *more* involved in her life and finding new people I have to fake the truth with. Especially her business partners.

But....I can't help it. I *do* want to meet her friends. I want to know every single part of her and do it all without the reputation and expectations that follow me around when people find out my net worth.

"Yeah, you should," Lilly responds quickly with a genuine smile. "They'll grill the heck out of you, though. Fair warning."

"I can handle it." I give a slightly cocky shrug.

"Well...I'd love for you to meet them. When we're not

working, we usually hang out at Coconuts. It's sort of a random, indoor-outdoor bar a few blocks from here. So maybe I'll bring you along one of these days." The playful wink she shoots me makes my body ache for her.

"I'd be honored," I tease.

"What about you? Who do you hang out with? I know you said you only recently moved here, but hopefully you've made some friends."

Yeah, my slightly douchey but very lovable finance bros from Cornell...that's who I hang out with. Well, that's who TJ the hedge fund manager hangs out with. TJ the hedge fund *trimmer* probably would roll with a different crowd.

"I've got a couple buddies around here," I say vaguely. "But you're by far the best friend I've made so far."

She gives an exaggerated stage gasp. "Did you just...*friendzone* me?"

I laugh heartily. "Oh yeah. I think it's pretty obvious that I don't have any kind of attraction to you whatsoever."

"Oh, good." She fake wipes her forehead. "Whew. That's a relief. Because I have absolutely *no* attraction to you, so I'm glad we're on the same page."

I bite back a laugh and hold her electrifying gaze. "Thank goodness."

In an effort to not have this unforgettably awesome day and evening come to an end, I take a quick breath and ask, "Do you want to go back to—" But before I can finish the sentence with "my place," I realize...oh crap.

She can't come to *my* place. My place is the mansion on San Marino Island.

"Or I can just take you home," I add quickly. "If you'd prefer that."

The thought of that completely sucks, but I've gotten myself into a nasty pickle here.

"Well..." Lilly lifts a shoulder and smiles with a spark in her eye. "I think we're pretty close to my condo, if you want to come hang at mine."

Relief hits me like a train, and I try not to be too obvious about how blessedly perfect that suggestion is. "Oh, yeah, I forgot you live right near here. That sounds great." I keep my eyes locked with hers as I nod toward the bar. "I'll get the check."

"Okay." She smiles.

As we walk out of Ben's and head down the street, the air is slightly cooler, with the tiniest hint of a chill dancing around us.

Lilly's hair bounces and billows in the wind, her eyes wide and joyful as she turns to me and lifts her head up to meet my eyes.

The painfully adorable sundress she has on is flowing around her long, slender legs, and the bright colors and flowers of it match her vibe perfectly.

We chat and laugh as we walk down the street, which is bustling with people and music and the constant hum of city noise.

It's different than the New York City hustle, though. It's...brighter. Warmer. Happier. I know I'm only here for a season, but...dang. I could really stay here.

With...her.

Except I can't. And that reality stabs me pretty hard.

"Sometimes I wish Miami was on the west coast so we got the sunset instead of the sunrise," Lilly muses, our hands locked together between us, swinging as we go.

"What's wrong with sunrises?"

"What's wrong with them is that they occur when I'm sleeping." She laughs. "That's what."

"Fair enough," I say.

"I always tell myself I'm gonna get up and go for a sunrise run on the beach. Two years I've been telling myself that."

I chuckle and shake my head. "Doesn't happen, does it?"

"Never. Not once."

As we laugh and walk, we pass by a fancy-looking restaurant with outdoor seating and lots of plants and arches and vines decorating the tables by the street. It catches my eye, and suddenly I recognize it as the place I hung out with Blake and Dominic the other night. The place they said they always go to. The place that...

Oh crap, they're there.

My heart rate kicks up a notch as we get closer to the restaurant, and I can confidently confirm that Dominic and Blake are sitting at one of the outdoor tables with their wives, laughing and sipping wine, sharing an appetizer.

They cannot see me. If they notice me, they will inevitably want to chat, and inevitably give everything away and make me look like the absolute worst person alive.

"Hey..." I grab Lilly's waist and pull her close to me, turning toward the street near a crosswalk. "Let's go to the other side of the road."

"Oh, but...we don't need to cross right now, we can just—"

"Yeah, we do." As soon as the light changes, I keep my

grasp on her and hurry down the street, praying I don't hear my name called behind me.

"Are you sure?" Lilly asks with a confused laugh. "I really don't think we have to—"

"We definitely do." I nod, keeping my face hidden as we speed walk past the restaurant, now on the other side of the road. "Let's hurry. We should hurry."

"Okay, what the heck is going on with you right now?" she asks with crossed arms and a playful tone. "You're acting weird."

"No, no." I wave a dismissive hand and shake my head as we finally turn a corner around the block and get out of their line of sight. "I'm fine. It's all good."

"Come on." She rolls her eyes and laughs as we cross another street and get closer to her neighborhood. "Tell me what that was all about."

Nerves prickle in my chest and I try to choose my words carefully. I've never been a liar or fake or anything but my total authentic self. This stuff does not come naturally to me. Plus, I really don't want to lie to her.

"I just..." I let out a breath. "I saw someone back there that I really didn't feel like talking to. I didn't want them to notice me. It's a long story, I'll spare you the details."

"Ooh, drama." She gasps with a soft laugh as we finally reach the parking area for her building. "Please don't spare anything, I must know all. Was it an ex?"

"Uh, no, no. Not an ex or anything like that."

"I thought you didn't know anyone here, though. Except for a couple buddies." She digs her keys out of her purse as we walk up a few stairs to get to the door of her ground floor condo.

"Like I said, it's a weird and long story and I definitely don't need to get into it." I open the door for her after she unlocks it and smile brightly. "Let's just chill and have a good time."

"All right..." She holds up her hands as if surrendering. "I won't pry."

Shame grips my chest knowing it might hurt her to think I'm keeping a secret. But I am keeping a secret...a big, fat pile of them now, actually.

I should tell her. I should just spit it out, standing here in the living room of her condo, I should just come clean and say the truth and accept the inevitable fact that she'll never want to see me or talk to me ever again.

But then she turns around. Those big blue eyes glimmer and that thick, shiny blonde hair falls around her delicate face like a glowing frame. Her soft laugh sounds like music and her very presence makes me feel less guarded.

I know, theoretically, I'm being totally fake. But when I'm with her...it's the most real I've ever felt. I don't want to let that go. Not...yet.

"So, this is my little abode." She bounces on her toes and grins widely, gesturing at the space around her.

The living room is decorated with a big tapestry on the wall and a large array of house plants. The windows have pink, lace curtains hanging around them and there's a wall entirely devoted to photographs hanging in frames.

There are blankets and throw pillows and colorful, mismatched furniture that seems to fit her almost as well as that sundress.

"It's so..." I shake my head and give an easy laugh. "*You.*"

"Thank you." She tilts her head. "It's my sanctuary, that's for sure."

"Look at all these..." I say softly, walking over to the picture wall and slowly studying each happy little snapshot. "Miss Popular, huh?"

She laughs sharply and stands next to me. "Yeah, except if you look closely, you'll see the same four people in almost every one of those pictures."

"You guys are really close."

She raises a shoulder. "We're like sisters." She heads back over to the kitchen, which is connected to the living room. "You want a drink or anything? I may or may not only have ridiculously cheap wine so...sorry not sorry for that. Oh, I know! We could order pizza." Her voice trails off as she rummages through the kitchen.

I can't help but look down and smile at the situation. At the...modesty of it. Dating, for me, has always been about the fanciest restaurants, the most expensive meals, the bougiest bottle of champagne, and inevitably the most forced conversation and passive agendas.

But now...I'm here. Ordering pizza and sitting on a couch of a one-bedroom condo with cheap wine. And it feels like I'm living in the world I've always been missing.

It's not that I don't like having money, and it's not that I'm ungrateful for my wealth. I just wish it didn't make people—women in particular—form such strong opinions of me. Or, worse...have ulterior motives.

Not Lilly. I don't think she has a manipulative bone

anywhere in that perfect little body. To her, I'm a down-to earth blue-collar worker. And she adores it.

And I adore her. And all I want is to live in this little escape forever, even though I know I can't.

"Here." She hands me a glass of white wine. "My finest bottle of seven-dollar Chardonnay, courtesy of Bianca's birthday party a couple weeks ago."

I raise the glass and smile at her. "I wouldn't have it any other way."

THIRTEEN

LILLY

He's holding back. He's holding back and I want to know why. I want to know who put those walls up and what makes him so guarded and how come I can't quite seem to get a read on him?

The curiosity about the enigma of a man sitting in front of me is completely overwhelming, but hesitations have never held me back before, so...why start now? If there are some layers that need to be peeled back...well, I'm all here for the peeling.

Aubrey would tell me to analyze every little detail of his behavior and demeanor and take the questions as potential red flags, add them into a pro/con list, and to a technical and detailed analysis of if I should continue things. But I'm...not Aubrey. Risks don't scare me. And in the case of TJ...they intrigue me.

"Is it everything you hoped it would be?" I ask with a

laugh, nodding at the glass of embarrassingly crappy wine he's holding.

I clean up the pizza box from our Domino's delivery which we already devoured, and head back into the living room.

"It's...ten out of ten." He shakes his head and smiles, swirling the glass around. "I think I have a new favorite wine."

"They're on BOGO a lot at Costco," I tease, gesturing for us to sit down on the couch, hopefully close to each other.

"Well, I'll have to go stock up then, won't I?" He winks at me as he adjusts one of my many patterned throw pillows to sit down on the sofa.

I smile at him, his gaze deep and enchanting as he inches closer. His gorgeous lips are curved in an easy, natural half-smile, begging to be kissed.

I want to know everything about him right this second, but I can obviously tell he doesn't really roll that way. I guess he's just a slow burn type of guy, so I'll take what I can get.

I'm dying to ask about the totally bizarre incident on the way here, as if he was hiding from someone, but I don't want to pry. Clearly, he had no interest in elaborating on that, and I'll have to just take a chill pill and let him tell me on his own time.

"So, have you started again?" I ask.

"Started what?" He draws back, furrowing his brow with confusion.

"Painting again, silly!" I nudge his arm playfully, using

it as an excuse to scoot even closer to him on the couch so that our legs are touching.

"Oh, god." He rolls his eyes and bites back a laugh. "You're still on that?"

"Heck yeah I'm still on it. And I'm gonna stay on it until you get to whippin' that brush around, or...whatever the hip lingo for painting is."

He runs a hand through his hair, making it just tousled enough to be somehow even sexier than before. "I don't think that's something I have any interest in anymore. I mean..." He shrugs dismissively. "I was just a little kid when I was into painting."

"But you loved it! You said it was your favorite thing to do," I say with encouragement.

"Well, yeah, when I was seven." He lowers his gaze and gives me a teasing smile. "Do you still love to do the things you enjoyed when you were seven? Am I gonna find a hidden stash of Barbie dolls somewhere in this condo?"

"Okay..." I laugh and shake my head, adjusting my position on the couch cushions. "But that's different. Painting isn't *just* for children. Barbies are. Most of the time."

"Why do you care so much that I paint again?" he asks softly, searching my face.

I toy with a loose thread on the edge of my throw blanket, pondering the question. "Because you lit up when you talked about it. I could tell just the thought of it made you happy, even if it was the bittersweet kind of happy. Because of..." My voice trails off.

"My mom," he finishes steadily.

"Yeah."

He puffs out a breath, sipping the garbage wine. "I don't know. To be totally honest, I haven't talked to anyone about that stuff..." He waves a hand. "Painting or my mom or any of it...in a really long time. It's not really something I tell people."

I hug my knees up to my chest and rest my chin on them. "Well, you told me."

"Well...you're not just..." He lowers his voice. "People."

"I'm not?" I cock my head and laugh softly.

"No, you're...different. Somehow I feel like I can really be myself with you." He smiles and glances down. "It's weird, I just...I don't know. I feel like opening up to you is right. Like, you get me."

The words make my heart sing, and give me hope that those walls will continue to slowly come down, and I can truly get to know...and possibly love...the real TJ.

"Well, I'm glad," I say softly, moving closer to him.

"Me too," he whispers.

Before I know it, his lips are on mine, making me feel like I'm floating up onto a cloud, and time and space and earth melt away. My heart squeezes and heat floods me as I hold his chiseled jawline in both of my hands.

We kiss back and forth, tasting each other's lips and letting our hands hold each other like they were meant to do just that.

I smile against his lips as the intensity builds, my chest airy and light and swarmed with butterflies.

"Cheap wine..." he whispers, his voice raspy and low as he kisses me between words. "Pizza...and you."

I giggle softly.

"I think this is just about the best night I've ever had." The sincerity in his voice sends me soaring.

"I could not agree more." I run my hand through his hair, pulling back for a second to truly appreciate how devilishly handsome he is, fully drinking in his perfection. "And thanks for joining me at the zoo today."

"I loved every second, Lilly." He runs his thumb along my cheekbone, making me feel more seen and admired and adored than ever before.

I lean into him, his strong arms holding me, wrapping me up in a blanket of safety and attraction. We kiss more, eventually ending up laying down on the couch, snuggled under a blanket, hidden from the rest of the world.

I know things could go further physically tonight and... dang, I really want them to. But I get the vibe that TJ is someone who likes to take things slow. And I feel so strongly for him, I think that's the best way to go about this.

Besides, I want to feel like he's fully opened up to me before we take that next step toward intimacy. And even though he's genuine and real and brimming with authenticity, I want to get to where I don't think he's holding anything back. Anything at all.

'Cause I sure am not.

"If you could spend a week one place in the entire world..." He runs a hand through my hair, toying with it between his fingers. "Where would it be?"

I hesitate for a second, wrapped up underneath his arm with my head laying on his chest as it rises and falls.

"Don't think too hard," TJ says. "Just...first place that comes to mind."

"Alaska," I blurt out, without thinking too hard.

"Shut up," he snorts, shaking his head as he stares up at the ceiling.

"What?" I tilt my chin up to meet his gaze and wrinkle my nose. "What's wrong with Alaska? Lots of people go there."

"I don't know." He chuckles softly, the sexy, low sound of it echoing through my ears. "Nothing's wrong with it, necessarily. I just expected, like, Hawaii or Fiji or something."

"Yeah, but..." I curl onto my back, lacing my fingers through his. "I already live somewhere super tropical and beachy. If I'm going to vacation, I would want to experience something totally different, you know? But, mostly I really, really want to see the Northern Lights."

He ponders this, gently stroking the side of my hand with his thumb. "Yeah, that's a good point actually. I would love to see the Northern Lights, now that you mention it."

"What about you?" I ask. "Have you traveled a lot?"

He hesitates a bit, swallowing visibly.

I try to push away that same nagging feeling that there's...something going on. Something he's not telling me. I can't imagine what it could be, but I also can't shake the feeling that there's...something.

"I, uh..." TJ waves a hand. "I've been here and there. Nothing too crazy."

"Have you been to Alaska?" I ask, grinning.

"I have not," he says with certainty, making my fleeting nagging feeling go away as quickly as it came. "And I can't say I've ever had a wildly burning desire, but I can see the appeal. Aurora Borealis and all that."

"It's got to just be the most magical thing on the planet." I sigh, fantasizing about the natural wonder. "Plus, Alaska in general. You can literally do dogsled tours. Like...

come on." I laugh and wave my hands with enthusiasm. "Is that not the coolest thing ever?"

"Maybe one day we can go to Alaska. And see the Northern Lights."

The word "we" slips off his tongue like it was the most easy and natural thing for him to say.

My heart does another little kick, and I try to stifle the insanely excited smile that's yanking at my cheeks, making me feel like a schoolgirl who just got asked to the prom.

"Yeah," I whisper. "Maybe we can."

One step at a time, one piece at a time, one moment at a time...I am falling for this man. And for the first time in forever...I'm loving the ride.

FOURTEEN

TJ

"You stayed over at her place?" Blake's shocked voice comes through the phone call with a hysterical laugh. "Dude."

"Yeah, but nothing happened," I insist with an eye roll, holding the phone to my ear as I pace back and forth through the backyard, making circles around the giant pool.

"Nothing happened?" Dominic, who's also on our three-way phone call, asks. "Nothing at all?"

"Okay, not *nothing*," I admit, pushing away the warm, happy, unfamiliar feeling that grips me every time I think about her. A feeling, of course, that is paired with an equally intense sense of regret and shame and dread about the fact that she has no idea who I truly am because I've taken the little "mistaken identity" bit way too far. But there's no going back now.

"So you slept with her?" Blake clarifies.

"No, I didn't. We didn't have sex, I slept on the couch.

It was just late and we'd had some wine and she asked if I wanted to stay."

"And your answer was," Dominic interjects, "yes, but on the couch."

I chuckle and run a hand through my hair as I continue pacing. "Yes. Look, I really want to take this slow and try to figure everything out before we get to...that level. I don't want to hurt her."

"Teej...I love you, bro," Blake says. "But with all the love and respect in the world...you're way past the point of hurting her. You took what could have been solved with one sentence the first time you met, and turned it into a catastrophic lie."

I clench my jaw, hating how painfully right he is.

"I just..." I let out an audible groan. "I had no idea I would like her this much. Dang...if I had known she was going to turn out to be the freaking woman of my dreams, I probably would have chosen a different course of action."

"You thought it would just be a fling..." Dominic suggests.

"I didn't think it would be anything!" I exclaim, switching the phone to my other ear as I splash the edge of the pool with my bare foot. "Wanna know what I thought? I thought there was an adorable, gorgeous girl standing in my front yard who accidentally thought I was the gardener, because she was expecting Theodore Rinehart to look like my father. I thought it was cute, and endearing. I played along. Next thing I know I'm catching mad feelings and sleeping on her couch."

They both stay quiet for a few seconds on the phone, processing the hot mess that is my current life.

"Stuff happens, man, but this...wow." Dominic blows out a breath. "This is pretty next level crazy."

"Can't you just come clean?" Blake asks. "Just throw it all out there. What's she gonna say—'Oh no, I don't want you anymore because I found out that you're a billionaire'? Come on, bro. She might not be super materialistic, but she's still a human."

"It doesn't matter at this point. It's way too late." I finally stop pacing and sit down on one of the outdoor sofas underneath the awning of the patio. "She could find out that I'm Superman, and she'd still hate me for keeping such an enormous secret and lying to her. Besides, she's horrified by people like me. Fully funded by Dad's money, given a fat trust fund and handed a million-dollar job just because of my family name." I rest my head in my hands, feeling defeated and lost. "As odd and bizarre and backward as it sounds...she'd never want me if she knew all of that."

"How have you been able to actually talk to her?" Blake asks. "Like, how does your job and money and background just...not come up?"

"I don't know. I dodge the questions I can't answer. But for the most part, I just like getting to know her. I could listen to her talk forever. And, when I take out the money and the work and all of that...I really am completely myself with her. More than I've ever been with anyone that I've dated. That's what I was trying to tell you guys when I first mentioned this whole dumpster fire. It's just so...refreshing. I can just *be*."

Dominic clicks his tongue and groans loudly. "But... you're not a gardener. You're a billionaire hedge fund manager."

"Thanks for the update," I mutter sarcastically.

"I do not envy you, my dude." Blake sighs sympathetically. "I do not envy you."

"What should I do?" I flop back onto the couch, holding a hand over my eyes to block the blinding, mid-morning sun.

"Have you told your dad?" Dominic asks.

"Oh, absolutely not." I lay my head back on a cushion and tuck my arm underneath it, holding the phone up with my other hand.

"Maybe you should," Blake says, his voice rising with enthusiasm. "TJ, you and your dad are super tight. I feel like he's a wise man with solid advice."

"Yeah," I snort. "Solid investing advice. Solid financial advice. Solid career building advice. He'd be so stunned by this entire insane situation, I don't even know how I'd begin to explain it to him."

"It might be worth a shot," Dom adds.

They're right about the fact that my dad and I are really close. I was basically raised by a single dad after my mom left when I was nine, and I've loved following in his footsteps. He's inspiring and interesting and freakishly brilliant. And, of course, he has great advice. But...not about things like this.

He's great with lectures and motivational speeches and enthusiastic pep talks. I don't know how he'd handle this particular crap show, and I have to admit that I definitely have a fear of disappointing him. Or worse...pissing him off.

"I'll think about it," I say to my friends on the phone. "But for now, I've gotta get back to work. Enough dating drama for the day."

"You brought the drama on yourself, brother." Blake chuckles heartily. "But I'm all here for it."

"Yeah, yeah." I roll my eyes and smile to myself. "Grab your popcorn and enjoy the mess that is my life."

"Talk to you guys later," Dom says, hanging up.

"Peace. Good luck, TJ," Blake adds.

"Thanks," I let out on a breath, dropping the phone onto the couch next to me after the call ends.

I am in so deep. So, so, dangerously freaking deep. And the worst part is, even in the midst of the craptastic situation and inevitable catastrophic blowup that this is all going to cause...

I still can't stop thinking about her. I still can't shake those dang jitters and that feeling of hope and happiness and excitement for what's next.

Those blue eyes live in my mind absolutely rent free, and I frequently find myself counting the days until her next cleaning day or our plans to see each other.

I'm falling in love and living a lie all at once, and it's as exciting as it is terrifying.

FIFTEEN

LILLY

"There's our little bride-to-be!" Bianca sings as I walk into the office with a carrier full of lattes and an obviously bright smile on my face.

"Oh, would you stop it?" I roll my eyes playfully and squeeze around what little room there is between our desks, passing out the coffees. "We've only been on a few dates."

"That's a few more than any of the rest of us," Meredith remarks, arching her brow.

"Yeah, girl." Cici sips the latte, wrapping her hands around the cup and eyeing me. "You were MIA on Saturday."

"We went to the zoo, and the..." My voice trails off and I shrug nonchalantly as I slide my desk chair out and sit down. "We hung out."

"You *hung out*?" Bianca walks over to my desk and places both her hands on it, staring at me with intensity.

Aubrey gasps, listening in. "Oh my gosh. Did you..."

Meredith squeals. "You had..." She lowers her innocent little voice to a whisper, mouthing the word *sex*.

"No!" I laugh and wave a hand, dismissing their rapid assumptions. "We didn't. We could have, but...not yet." I let out a deep sigh. "I don't know, you guys. This feels... real. This feels like it could seriously be something."

"Are you scared?" Aubrey asks, looking over her laptop screen.

"Not really. That's the crazy part. I know I could get hurt, but I don't care. I trust him." I decide to omit the little detail about me thinking there could be something he's hiding. It's not that I think he's a shady person, and I definitely don't take him for a liar. He is absolutely one of the most genuine people I've ever met.

And maybe it's just my own cautionary voice nagging me in the back of my mind that there is something he's holding back. Either way, it's not enough to take away any of my excitement and joy.

"Well, we are all beyond happy for you, love." Cici grins at me brightly.

"We wanna meet him!" Meredith exclaims, gathering her flowing brown waves of hair and pushing them all over one shoulder.

"Actually, he was saying the same thing." I smile, moving my chair back in the six inches of space I've got between my desk and the wall. "Of course I've talked endlessly about you girls, and he wanted to meet you all. I might invite him out this week, if you guys are cool with that."

Bianca gasps and claps her hands together. "I am ready to grill this man into oblivion."

I glare at her playfully. "Easy, B. I *like* this one. Let's not scare him away, please?"

She raises a sassy brow and folds her arms across her chest. "You know I'm kidding, Lil. I'd love to meet TJ the Gardener."

"Let's do it." Aubrey skims through the schedule that's never not right in front of her. "Wednesday night? At Coconuts?"

"As if we ever go anywhere else," Cici adds with an easy laugh.

"Cool, I'll tell him." I pull out my phone and don't even attempt to hide the smile that yanks at my cheeks as I write the text to TJ.

"Meeting the boyfriend..." Cici shimmies her toned arms and giggles. "Big stuff happening here, ladies."

"I don't know if I'd use the word boyfriend just yet..." I bite back a smile.

"Oh yeah? What would you call it, then?" Bianca asks with a hair flip.

"I don't know." I shrug and lean back into my chair, swiveling it back and forth. "Something like...almost boyfriend. I guess."

"You said he stayed over..." Meredith widens her gaze. "Right?"

"Yes, but like I told you guys, he slept on the couch. It was just getting late and I had driven that day and honestly I didn't feel like driving him back."

"Where does he live?" Aubrey asks, perpetually interested in logistics. "Is it super far from you? Or close by?"

"He lives..." I catch myself, glancing out the window as the wheels in my brain start turning pretty rapidly. "Huh."

"What?" Bianca demands.

"What is it, Lil?" Meredith angles her head, studying me.

"I..." I give a dry laugh, a bit embarrassed to admit this. "I don't actually know where he lives. When we went to the zoo, he told me to just pick him up from a coffee shop, so that's what I did."

"Have you asked him?" Cici asks.

"No..." I shake my head, casually lifting a shoulder. "I haven't. I guess it's just never come up in conversation."

"Are you worried?" Aubrey asks me tenderly. "You look pale and...concerned."

"No, no." I force a smile and flick my wrist dismissively. "Not at all. I just never asked, but there was never a real reason for him to mention it. I'm just being weird."

"You guys." Aubrey's voice of excitement blessedly takes the attention off of me and my potentially house-less boyfriend. Er, almost boyfriend.

"What?" Bianca squeezes through the tight space between desks, craning her neck to see Aubrey's computer screen.

"I wanna see." Cici stands up and leans over.

Meredith does the same, and I slide out of my desk and walk over to find out what made Aubrey gasp and squeal.

"It's Zachary Thorne!" she exclaims, pointing to an article headline on her computer. "The rumors are true. Apparently it's been confirmed that he's officially closing on that lot in South Beach. It looks like he's set to move in in about six or seven months. he's picked building a house in South Beach and is going to be moving in, like, seven months! It's a fatty, too. Thirteen thousand square feet of messy, dirty, Solo cup-ridden real estate."

"Heck to the yes!" Bianca pumps a fist in the air.

"Okay, now that it's official, we definitely have to jump on this guy's business," Cici agrees, fascinated as she skims the details of the house listing.

"Or jump on the guy himself," Bianca nudges me with a teasing wink. "I mean...are you kidding? He's a god."

"He's a real looker, that's for sure," Aubrey adds, blowing up the thumbnail picture of him attached to the listing.

"Those eyes. Wow," I have to admit, studying the familiar face of a rock star heartthrob who's been a house-hold name for the last few years. "I can't believe he's actually moving here. I mean, I know we'd read something about it a couple weeks ago, but you know how celebrity rumors are. I never thought it could actually happen. He's *loaded*."

"And gorgeous." Bianca does a happy dance.

"And...*messy*." Aubrey flicks her brows up and down deviously.

Seemingly all at once, the four of us realize that Meredith is hanging back at her desk, exceptionally quiet and blatantly uninterested in Zachary Thorne and his messy mansion.

"Mer, what's wrong?" I ask, walking over to her.

Her big, brown eyes look bothered and her body language is...tense. "Nothing. I just..." She swallows. "I don't see why we need to get business from some famous jerk like that."

"Girl, are you crazy?" Bianca, not *quite* as sensitive and

sympathetic, but of course she means well, struts over to Meredith's desk. "He's a celebrity. This would be by far our most high-profile account."

"It really is huge, Mer," Aubrey adds.

"So what?" Meredith crosses her arms. "We already have a billionaire." She points at me. "Lilly's account. Billionaire, like, with a B. Why do we need some stupid, tattooed, angsty bad boy who can play a couple guitar riffs and sleep with a thousand groupies?"

"Something tells me you're not a Zachary Thorne fan girl..." Cici offers a soft laugh.

"No kidding," I snort. "What's so upsetting about this guy, Meredith?"

"I mean, just..." She gestures angrily toward Aubrey's computer screen, where the handsome face and shaggy blond hair is still blown up and zoomed in. "Look at him! He's bad news. He's just a typical musician bad boy, and we don't need his business."

"Mer, I love you and totally respect that this isn't the crowd you personally want to be associated with," I say gently, leaning against the side of her desk. "But we've got to get him for the company."

"We could generate enough new profit to finally move into a bigger, brighter office," Aubrey suggests, her eyes lighting up.

"See?" I ask Meredith encouragingly. "This is gonna be great for us."

"What's this really about?" Bianca asks skeptically, focusing her attention on the slumping Meredith.

"Nothing," she answers quickly, brushing off the question. "I just think he's bad news and we should stay away."

"I mean, come on, Mer." Bianca raises a shoulder. "It's not like you've *met* the guy."

Meredith's eyes flash and darken, and she stands up and grabs her bag, swinging it over her shoulder. "You're right, I haven't. I don't know him at all." She shakes her head and gives an obviously forced smile. "I'm just being weird. But...I've got to go. I'm supervising a housekeeping at eleven. That rich family in Coral Gables."

"Okay, have fun." I grin and give her a wave.

"Love you, Virgin Mer," Bianca calls after her as she makes her swift exit.

"Okay, is it just me"—Cici angles her head slowly—"or was Meredith like *really* weird about this rock star guy?"

Aubrey sips her coffee and shrugs. "I think she's just intimidated by a guy like that."

"I mean, shoot, so am I," I offer lightly. "He's, like, seriously famous. And she's not wrong about the bad boy thing."

"Yeah, and I think that just freaks her out," Bianca adds. "Zachary Thorne certainly does have a reputation."

"He also has deep pockets, which I care a heck of a lot more about," Aubrey adds with a wiggle of her brow.

"True that." I point at her and head back to my desk. "New office, here we come! Hopefully."

"We'll get there, Lil," Cici assures me.

"Even if it's not this year or next year or the one after that..." Bianca chimes in. "We're gonna get there."

Hope wells in my chest and I smile widely, turning back to my computer screen and taking a deep breath, feeling *even* more optimistic about life than usual. And, for me, that's saying something.

SIXTEEN

TJ

"It was...Bianca, right?" I smile and pass out the round of drinks I bought as I make eye contact with a pretty, feisty, brown-eyed Latina girl.

"You're a fast learner," she says approvingly, taking the drink from me and raising the straw to her lips. "I'm impressed."

"Thank you, I try," I tease, glancing around to take in the scenery in a place I've definitely never been before.

Coconuts, despite its relatively uninteresting name, resembles a cheesy-yet-quirky and slightly endearing tiki bar, with parts of it being outside and decorated with lights and flowers and all sorts of Hawaiian themes. It's on a low rooftop, and Lilly, her friends and I are all standing by the outdoor bar, enjoying the slight chill in the salty Miami breeze as the sun goes down.

With the comfort of knowing I'm definitely not going to run into anyone who knows or recognizes me here, I let myself relax and take a breath, enjoying the pureness of the little bubble that is Lilly McCarthy's world. And...enjoying even more so how well I fit into it.

"So, TJ..." Another friend addresses me, this one I believe to be Cici. A beautiful Asian girl, she's got long black hair, a warm and happy smile, and is in exceptionally good shape...like she might kick my ass at some point. Lilly mentioned that she's the athletic sports fan, and that checks out.

I make a mental note to watch out for her.

"Yeah?" I grin, glancing to my side at Lilly, who is deep in chatty conversation with Aubrey and Meredith, the other two girls.

"Lilly said you're a gardener? You work for that Rinehart billionaire guy?"

No, I am *that Rinehart billionaire guy.*

A small part of me just wants to let go and scream the truth out from this rooftop, but the intoxicating freedom is something I'm not willing to part with just yet. Or ever.

"That's me," I say, almost laughing to myself about how, well, that isn't technically a lie.

That is me.

"Do you think it's so weird that Lilly hasn't met him?" Bianca leans close, joining in the conversation. "She's been supervising that account for a few weeks now and still hasn't even met the guy."

I swallow and take a breath to respond, but before I have the chance to open my mouth and say something, Aubrey, Lilly, and Meredith have all joined us in a little circle, chiming in.

"He's paying us and everything." Aubrey shrugs and

lifts her drink, looking up to meet my gaze. "I've confirmed it all in the books and his electronic payments clear perfectly."

I know. I'm the one sending them.

"Yeah, it's..." I glance at Lilly, who's beaming at me. "It's definitely weird. I'm sure she'll meet him eventually."

"It's probably good that he's never come to the office," Lilly remarks.

"Oh, God." Bianca laughs and shakes her head. "Yes, that's definitely a plus. We do not need a billionaire seeing that shoebox."

"What do you mean?" I ask. "What's wrong with your office?"

"Well..." Lilly looks at me. "It's...tiny. It's the original office we rented when we could literally afford nothing else. And we just haven't had the budget, or honestly the logistic wherewithal, to get ourselves moved into a bigger spot."

"It's a nightmare." Bianca rolls her eyes. "Our desks are all smashed up against each other with absolutely no free space."

"And there's like one, tiny window," Lilly adds. "It sucks. But a new place isn't quite in the cards just yet."

"Dang..." I frown. "Hopefully soon through, right?"

"Fingers crossed." Bianca holds up her intertwined fingers.

"I know..." Lilly shakes her head. "It would be such a dream to have a big, bright office in some beautiful building."

"What's he like?" Meredith, a mousey, doe-eyed girl

who is exactly as Lilly describes, asks me. "The billionaire, I mean. Is he a jerk?"

Gosh, I hope not. But...maybe.

"He's, you know, fine." I shrug dismissively, itching to change the subject. "Pretty average dude."

"Yeah," Bianca laughs sharply, tilting her head back. "Just your average ole, run-of-the-mill billionaire."

The girls laugh and chat and thankfully divert the conversation away from me.

"Wanna know a secret?" Lilly whispers in my ear, standing on her tiptoes. Her cheeks are rosy and flushed, and her eyes are wide with a bright sparkle in them. That signature ponytail is dancing behind her back, with little strands of loose hair falling delicately around her face.

"I like secrets," I say, almost choking on the irony.

"See that bartender over there?" Lilly subtly nods her head in the direction of the guy working behind the bar. He's got to be in his mid-twenties, good-looking dude in a gruff sort of way.

"Yeah, what about him?"

She leans closer to my ear. "Bianca's been into him for the past two years. She's tried every means of flirtation in the book. And, believe me, she knows what she's doing."

I don't doubt it. Within two minutes of talking to Bianca, I could tell she was one of those naturally bubbly and flirtatious people.

"Has anything happened?"

"Not a thing," Lilly says. "And we're all so confused by it, especially B. Because when she wants something, specifically a guy, she gets him. That's just how she rolls. She's gorgeous and awesome and dudes love her. But even after two years, he will not take the bait." She laughs softly and shakes her head. "Drives her nuts."

"What are you two lovebirds whispering about?" Bianca walks over, wiggling her brows and crossing her arms.

"You," Lilly says matter-of-fact, making it pretty obvious that the concept of a *secret* doesn't hold much weight in this particular friend group.

"Me?" Bianca gives a stage gasp. "Not like I can blame you, but what's so interesting about me?"

Lilly waves a hand and rolls her eyes. "I was just filling TJ in on your perpetual case of unrequited love with Alec the Unattainable."

Bianca curls her lip and growls. "Drives me nuts, that boy."

I laugh and look at the two girls. "Have you tried just asking him out?"

"I should not be the one doing the asking," Bianca says insistently. "I don't ask. I get asked."

"Not by Alec," Lilly teases.

"He likes me." Bianca sips her drink. "I can tell he likes me. I just gotta figure out what his deal is."

I suck in a breath, wondering if Lilly has ever thought the same thing about me. Does she have any suspicions at all? I mean, she has to. Maybe she just thinks I'm guarded. Maybe she doesn't want to pry.

I almost wish she would ask. Hit me with some kind of un-dodgeable direct question and rip the Band-Aid off and end my stupid little escape fantasy gone way, way too far.

As the night goes on, I ease up even more, watching

Lilly laugh, her effervescence lighting up this bar brighter than the million tiki torches.

I get to know Bianca, Cici, Meredith, and Aubrey a bit, and I can start to really see their distinctive personalities the way that Lilly had described them. The girls seem more like sisters than friends in the way they interact and know each other, but then again, they're all radically different.

I find that I have something to talk about with each and all of them, and Lilly absolutely loves watching me be a part of the group and embrace the people closest to her.

It occurs to me that I love this world. I don't care that we're in a tacky bar with cheap drinks. Everyone is real, and genuine, and down to earth. And I fit in. If they knew about the real me...about the money...I would most definitely not fit in.

But they don't know. And I feel free.

For my entire life, women have come after me because they wanted to become a part of my world. Now that I know Lilly, all I want is to become part of hers.

SEVENTEEN

LILLY

"Oh my gosh, he is freaking adorable, Lil," Bianca squeals as we wash our hands side by side in the bathroom of Coconuts, smiling at our warm, rosy faces in the mirror, drenched in the happiness of the night.

"You guys really like him?" I grin hopefully.

"Dude." Cici pops out of a stall and flips on the sink, sliding me a look. "He is so cool. Such a chill and fun guy."

"I agree," Aubrey adds, fixing her shiny pink lip gloss in the mirror next to me. "I mean, how many guys can come out alone with five girls and fit in, like, perfectly?"

"And not just any five girls," Meredith points out, fixing her hair. "The five of us. Who are freaky connected and run solely on inside jokes and practically have our own language."

"He keeps up." Bianca wags a finger at me. "Not many of them can keep up. But he does. That's important."

"He does keep up with us, doesn't he?" I bite my lip and stifle a smile, the hope of it all squeezing in my chest.

"Now, I don't want to jinx anything," Aubrey says cautiously, dropping her tube of lip gloss back into her purse and smoothing the top of her hair. "But...I can really see him sticking around, Lil. Like...for a while."

I swallow, letting the giddy smile pull across my cheeks. "I can, too. Is that totally and completely insane?"

"Girl." Bianca levels her gaze with mine, leaning against the bathroom counter. "The only totally and completely insane thing here would be if you don't hold onto that man as tightly as you can."

I take a deep breath and one last look in the mirror before we all head out of the bathroom and back over to TJ, who didn't understand why we all had to go at the same time.

As if it isn't completely obvious that we went for the sole purpose of discussing him.

"Welcome back." He smiles softly, the sweet, sexy dimples around his lips forming a curve I'd like to kiss.

Maybe it's the alcohol or the beautiful weather or the way tonight has been even more perfect than I could have imagined, but I suddenly feel compelled to slide my hand around his back and tuck my head underneath his chin.

He holds me tight in response, giving me a squeeze.

My brain slips back to the surprise I planned for him later tonight, and excitement and nerves ripple through my chest.

I think he's going to absolutely love it. But...maybe not. I don't know. What I do know is that I really care about him, and I wanted to do something nice for him. And, selfishly, maybe start breaking down some of those sturdy walls.

I slip out of his grasp reluctantly in an effort to not have too much PDA in front of my friends, who are deep in conversation telling TJ some ridiculous story about me from grad school.

"She fell down the stairs?" he asks, choking on a laugh and glancing at me as I come back to earth and out of my fantasy land.

"Oh, God." I hold my palm to my forehead and shake my head. "Would you guys stop with this?"

"Come on, Lilly. It's hilarious and you know it," Bianca insists.

"Fine." I wave a hand and laugh. "Continue."

"So she tumbles down the stairs..." Bianca goes on, her hands moving wildly with her animated enthusiasm.

"Like a rag doll," Cici interjects with laughter.

"How much had you had to drink that night?" TJ asks me teasingly.

"Oh, plenty," Aubrey answers, holding up her hand. "That's the best part. She had an exam the next day, and she came out under the condition of"—she holds up air quotes—"only having a drink or two."

I giggle at the silly memory, watching TJ look at me with endearing amusement.

"So...she tumbles down the stairs...pizza in one hand and her high heels in the other. Night before an accounting exam, mind you." Bianca laughs as she tells the story, and I can't help but do the same.

"And I suck at accounting when I'm not hungover," I chime in, "so you can imagine how this went."

"But the most amazing part," Meredith jumps in, leaning forward. "She saved the pizza."

"No way." TJ laughs heartily.

"She really did." Cici nods, her eyes wide. "This girl is tumbling down the stairs at our apartment building, and her number one concern was to protect the box of pizza."

"And did the pizza make it unscathed?" I ask rhetorically, raising my brows with a grin.

"It sure did!" Aubrey exclaims.

"And now we all know where Lilly's true priorities lie."

"My financial accounting exam on the other hand..." I say slowly, giving an exaggerated cringe and leaning into him. "Let's just say it didn't fare quite as well as the extra-large pepperoni from the Italian Gator."

TJ laughs, shaking his head and smiling at me.

We laugh and drink and talk and laugh some more, and before I know it, it's after midnight.

"Hey..." I whisper into his ear, letting my fingers trace down the solid muscles of his back.

"Hey," he whispers back.

"Wanna go to my place? Like...now?"

His eyes light up and he nods quickly. "Uh, yeah. Let's go."

I assume he thinks we're going to sleep together. And who knows...we might. But that's definitely not the only fun thing I have planned for tonight.

EIGHTEEN

TJ

"What kind of surprise?" I ask for probably the tenth time as we slide out of the Uber, thank the driver, and walk up to Lilly's building.

"If I told you..." She turns around and leans forward, pulling on my hand as we head up the stairs. "It wouldn't be a surprise, now would it?"

"You're killing me," I groan as we walk down the hallway to her front door, her hair bouncing around her back. Her body looks absolutely beautiful in tight, dark jeans and a white tank top.

I hope the surprise involves removing some—or, all—of those clothes.

"Okay..." She grins widely as she turns the key in the door and it clicks open. "You ready?"

My mind whirrs with possibilities of what on earth this little surprise could be. "I think so?" I say with an uncertain chuckle.

"Come on." She leads me into the condo, flipping on a light switch as we reach the living room.

As soon as the room brightens up, I look around and process what I'm seeing. All of the furniture has been moved away to the edges of the room, making a huge space in the middle of the floor.

In that space, a big sheet has been laid out, and on it are two...

Canvases. With an assortment of paints and brushes.

Unexpected emotion catches in my throat as I stare at the scene in front of me. Instantly, I'm flooded with images of my mother, who was never without a paintbrush in her hand. That is, until I started seeing her once a year. And then not at all.

Lilly's holding her breath trying to read my silence, and she steps forward to me slowly. "I, um...I thought maybe we could paint." She lifts a shoulder. "But, I totally understand if you don't want to. You know what? This was...this was a stupid idea. It reminds you of your mom and I shouldn't have done this, I was just—"

"Lilly." I turn to her, taking her delicate chin in my fingers and tipping it up slightly to meet my eyes. "I absolutely love this."

"You do?" She lights up.

"I do." I lean down and give her a soft kiss, overwhelmingly touched by the sweetness of this gesture.

I didn't think I'd ever want to paint again. It was just a silly childhood hobby. But here...with Lilly...my heart feels light, and painting sounds really, really fun.

She kisses me back and smiles. "Oh, I'm so glad. I

didn't know if I was, like, overstepping or making you uncomfortable."

"No..." I whisper, brushing a strand of hair out of her face to lock my eyes with those brilliant blue oceans of hers. "You're perfect."

"Let's paint?" she asks softly with a big smile.

"Let's paint."

We sit down on the floor together, and I find it physically impossible to take my eyes off of her as she tucks her legs underneath her and situates all the paints and brushes, tying her hair into that adorable ponytail.

"What?" she asks, noticing my gaze.

"Nothing, I just..." I shake my head, forcing myself to look down at the blank canvas in front of me as I sit on the floor. "Nothing."

"What should we paint?" Lilly scoots closer to me, laughing softly. "I should warn you that my artistic abilities are...well, nonexistent."

"And mine have been dormant for the last twenty years, so I'm probably in the same boat." I study her for a second, leaning back on my palms as they press into the sheet she laid out on the ground. "The Northern Lights," I say, without really thinking about it.

"Huh?"

"That's what we should paint. The Northern Lights."

Those blue eyes widen and light up at the idea, and a sweet smile spreads across her face. "I love that. Here, I'll pull up a picture on my phone. Because I don't know about you, Picasso, but I'm gonna need at least a little bit of guidance."

I laugh and shake my head, gently running my fingers over the soft bristles of one of the unused paint brushes.

"We'll start with the night sky," I say, mixing a dark blue and spreading some streaks of it across the top of my canvas.

"Good idea." Lilly studies me and does the same. "And stars."

"Absolutely."

As we start coating our canvases in different shades of blue and black, I'm overcome with a familiar sense of calm. Lilly's soft giggle as she attempts to paint, her leg brushing up against mine every time she reaches for a new brush... the way everything feels.

I have to go out of my way to remind myself that reality even exists. When I'm with her...I'm seen. I'm understood. I'm...loved. And for the first time in my life, the reminders of my mom don't upset me and make me want to put up my guard. I'm used to just pushing away those memories, but right now, with Lilly...I don't mind them. I want to make new ones.

I can feel myself smiling down at the canvas, and I notice her studying me intently.

"I hope this didn't make you sad or anything..." she says slowly.

"You know...it doesn't. Not at all. And I'm kind of surprised that it doesn't, honestly."

She stays quiet, waiting for me to continue but clearly not wanting to push and pry.

"I...I don't know. I definitely never thought this is something I would do again. When my mom left..." I lift a shoulder. "It kinda messed with my head a lot, you know?"

"Of course," she whispers, gently setting a supportive hand on my leg. "I can't imagine."

"I felt pretty abandoned and definitely not wanted. But, I really can't complain," I add quickly. "Because I had an awesome dad."

"Okay, but you *can* complain." Lilly slides me a look, a level of understanding in her gaze. "Because that sucks. That must have been really painful."

"Yeah, it sucked. But we all have our struggles." I remember how Lilly told me what it was like growing up without much money, facing a whole slate of problems I never had to know. "I don't like to dwell on it now, and maybe that's why I never painted again after she left. It reminded me of her and brought all that pain back." I glide the brush on the canvas and let myself continue to dump out feelings that I haven't bothered to think or talk about in decades. "It put some serious walls up for me. I guess, I felt like after she left, I never wanted to be vulnerable with anyone. I never wanted to depend on anyone or be truly open."

Out of the corner of my eye, I can see her nodding slowly.

"Until..." I turn my head to meet her gaze, sparks flying. "Until now."

Lilly tilts her head as her eyes widen with surprise and intrigue. "Really?" The word is barely audible.

"Yeah," I say, surprised again by my own certainty and openness and how right everything feels in this moment. "I guess she left me feeling sort of empty. And I've ignored it all these years. But now, painting with you..." I meet her gaze, holding on to it as tightly as I can. "There's no more emptiness."

Joy visibly washes over her face as she leans close to me, gently running her fingers along my cheek. "I'm so happy to hear you say that. And thatnks for being so honest and...real."

"This was really special, Lilly," I say, relieved by the weight off my shoulders that I didn't even know I was carrying.

"I'm glad you like it." She smiles down at her canvas as she spreads her paint. "I just thought it would be fun. I could tell that when you talked about painting as a kid, it was something you really enjoyed." She turns and looks up at me, some loose strands of blonde falling around her cheeks. "I wanted to bring that feeling back for you. I didn't mean to make you talk about your mom but...I'm glad you did."

"Yeah. I am, too." I shake my head and give a half-smile. "But...why? Why did you want to do that for me?"

"Because I..." She focuses back down on the canvas. "I thought it would make you happy. I...I want to make you happy. I really...like you."

"I really like you, too."

After tonight? After all this? After one of the most thoughtful and adorable and kind things anyone has ever done for me? I think I more than "really like" her.

We chat and talk and paint, the darkness outside and the silence around us making it literally feel like no one— and nothing else—exists.

"Oh, crap," she whines with laughter, staring down at

an accidental brownish-orange blob that made its way into the center of her night sky.

"No worries..." I slide closer to her, taking the brush from her hand. "It'll be part of the Aurora Borealis. You can fix it."

"I definitely cannot." She runs her hand through her hair. "My Alaska scene is totally hopeless."

"That's okay." I turn and look at her, locking her gaze with mine. "I think it looks great."

"It looks like a baby vomited on my Northern Lights."

I laugh heartily, taking my brush and swiping a smudge of blue paint on the tip of her nose.

She gasps, drawing back as her mouth falls open with a shocked smile. "Oh no you did *not*."

I laugh and tap the brush again on her forehead.

"Oh okay." Lilly crosses her arms. "We're playing those games now, huh?"

"I think we are."

She dunks her brush in the bright green color and swipes it across my cheek.

I gasp and choke on laughter, grabbing a bigger brush to retaliate with some hot pink.

Lilly shrieks and gets up, jetting out of the living room, laughing wildly with every step. Her bare feet pad along the hardwood floor as her hair swings from side to side. She ducks behind the bedroom doorway, giggling.

"I'm gonna get you," I say through a laugh, wagging my pink-drenched brush in front of her.

"Not if I get you first." She whips her own brush out from behind her back and smears red and yellow all over my face.

"Oh man, you are out for blood, Lilly McCarthy!" I wrap my arms around her waist, effortlessly picking her up and holding her tightly against me as I lift her.

"Wait, wait, wait." She holds up a hand, and I lower her back down to the ground. "It's gonna stain our clothes. The paint."

I lean forward, holding her chin in my hand and planting a kiss on her lips. "Then I guess we'll just have to take them off, won't we?"

Her eyes widen as she draws back, a dirty smile pulling at her lips. "I guess we will."

Attraction grips me as the chemistry between us crackles and sparks like wildfire. I know she doesn't know the truth...I know it's going to ruin everything when she finds out.

But right now, nothing else feels real. Nothing else feels like it could possibly matter more than this night and this moment and this woman, and I'm going to hold on to it. I have to. Just...for tonight.

"Come here..." Lilly whispers, her gaze glimmering as she pulls me into the bedroom and shuts the door.

NINETEEN

LILLY

I can feel myself smiling before I even open my eyes, the gentle slivers of early morning light peeking through the curtains in my bedroom and barely waking me up.

I take a deep breath as I start to come alive, still feeling TJ's strong and loving and steady arms wrapped around me, just like they were when we fell asleep.

His chest rises and falls gently against my back, and I snuggle closer against him, never wanting the warmth and comfort and bliss of this moment to end.

Everything changed last night. Everything started to feel serious and big and...real. I'm falling for this guy. Hard. And getting lost in him emotionally and physically last night seemed to take those feelings to the next level.

Of course, there's always fear where love is concerned. But, deep down in my heart, I know it's mutual. I know he feels it, too. It's so obvious and reassuring and wonderful.

I'm not sure what the future holds, but today...waking up next to him...it looks pretty dang bright.

"Hi..." A raspy whisper startles me as he tightens his arms around my waist.

I turn around to face him, his hair tousled and his eyes sleepy. "Good morning," I whisper.

His enchanting gaze holds me and admires me as he gently strokes his thumb across my cheek.

I look into his eyes for a while, the moment feeling deeply intimate. There's something wavering in those brown eyes. Something...sad.

Worry zings through me, but I try not to instantly overthink.

"How are you feeling?" I ask, hoping maybe I'm just imagining his flash of concern.

"I'm..." TJ kisses my forehead, melting away any doubt. "I'm feeling great. Last night was absolutely incredible, in more ways than one."

I giggle and cuddle closer. "I'm glad you liked painting with me."

"I loved painting with you. I love everything with you."

His words tug at my heart, and warmth spreads through me. His hands hold me close and tight, and our bodies stay intimately intertwined under my puffy comforter.

He lets out a sharp sigh, making me worry again that something might be bothering him.

"What's wrong?" I ask, drawing back onto the pillow. "Is everything all right?"

"Lilly..." He says my name slowly, making worry and fear fire off rapidly in my brain.

Oh, no. Oh crap. What is he about to say? The answer should be no, nothing is wrong. Everything is great. I'm totally happy and I want to be with you.

"What is it?" I ask, unable to hide the hint of panic in my voice.

"I have to tell you something." TJ levels his gaze with mine, everything feeling suddenly so heavy and serious.

I swallow, nerves spiking. "What is it?"

He turns onto his back and sighs deeply. "Okay, I—"

Before he has a chance to continue, my phone starts buzzing like crazy, interrupting his sentence.

"Sorry." I turn over and grab it from my nightstand, seeing Cici's name as an incoming call. "I'll call her back." I decline the call and set the phone back down. "What's going on?"

"I'm trying to figure out how to word this..."

Buzzing again.

Dang it, Ci! Not now!

I pick up the phone with a grunt, this time to see a text from her.

Please get to the office now! Emergency!

"What the heck?" I ask to myself, frustrated.

"What is it?" TJ pushes up onto his elbows, angling his head.

"It's..." I wave a hand and squeeze my eyes shut. "It's Cici. She's begging me to get to the office as soon as possible. Evidently there's some sort of emergency, although I can't imagine what it could possibly be that's so urgent..."

"You should go," TJ says, offering a smile.

"No, no. I'll deal with it later." I set the phone face down. "Please, tell me what you wanted to tell me."

"It's nothing, really."

"It doesn't seem like nothing." I scoot closer and search his face, not quite able to get a read on him right now.

He clenches his jaw and then looks at me, his eyes deep and sincere. "I just wanted to tell you that I..." He takes a breath, making my heart flutter. "I had a wonderful time last night. I That's all I wanted to say."

Happiness tingles in my chest, and I can't even try to stifle my cheesy grin. My body feels warm and light and everything feels right. "I did, too."

"Good."

"Good." I lean forward and kiss him, squeezing my eyes shut and letting the joy and excitement of the moment wrap around me.

"Are you sure that was it?" I ask gently. "I feel like there's something on your mind."

"I'm just..." He swallows. "A little deeper in my feels than I thought I would be."

"Isn't that a good thing?" I ask playfully.

His gaze darkens and moves away from mine. "Yeah. It is. I promise."

Another freaking crazy phone buzz jolts me.

"What could possibly be happening at your office?" TJ asks, running a hand through his bed head and laughing softly.

I groan and roll my eyes, reaching for the phone to read another panicky text from Cici.

Lil, please. I'm alone in the office and I seriously need you here NOW.

"She's alone at the office?" I ask to myself softly,

rereading the message. "Oh, right. Everyone else is out on client calls right now."

"Is she okay?" TJ asks, his genuine concern for my friend touching.

"Yeah..." I say slowly, a bit unsure. "I mean, I think so. I don't know, though. Cici is tough as nails, so something would have to be seriously wrong if she's this freaked out."

"Do you want me to go with you? If there's something unsafe, you shouldn't be going alone." TJ sits up, concern in his eyes.

"Hang on..." I dread the idea of leaving this bed, so I grab my phone and call Cici to see what the heck all the craziness is about.

It rings and rings and rings and then goes to voicemail.

"How is she going to text me but not pick up the phone?" I roll my eyes, a bit more concern rising in my throat.

I fire off a quick text to Bianca and Meredith, even though I know they're out at client meetings. Maybe one of them can address this, but I doubt it. I don't want anything to get screwed up with a client, and Cici and I are the only two not out on calls right now.

"Seriously, Lilly." TJ places a strong hand on my leg, making me melt a little. "I don't want you going there alone if there's some kind of danger. Let me come with you."

A tendril of worry crawls up my spine, and I try giving Cici another phone call. This time, she picks up.

"Lil!" she says frantically.

"Cici!" I hold the phone tight to my ear. "Are you okay? Are you in danger? TJ is going to come to the office with me if there's something—"

"No, no, no..." she says quickly and dismissively. "No that is totally not necessary. I just need you alone. I'm not in danger, but I really do need you to get here now. Please, Lilly."

"Can you just tell me what's going on?" I ask, sharing an apologetic look of confusion with TJ.

"Please just get here I need you." And with that, she hangs up.

"So...no imminent danger?" TJ asks. "You're sure?"

"Yeah, it must be...a work thing?" I cock my head, trying to figure this out. "She's pretty insistant that I get there, though. And she is alone..."

"You better go," TJ says gently. "You're sure you're fine on your own?"

"Yes, positive. She'd tell me if it was something unsafe. I am so, so sorry..." I shake my head and give him one last kiss.

"It's okay. You're a great friend, they're lucky to have you."

The compliment warms as I reluctantly get up and start changing my clothes. "In a perfect world, I'd stay in bed with you all day."

TJ moans and leans back onto the headboard. "That would be a dream."

I rush around to brush my teeth, comb my hair, and swipe on some mascara; all the while my phone is still vibrating with more all caps texts coming in.

"I don't know what on earth this emergency could possibly be," I mutter, hopping around to get my foot into a low black wedge. "Cici's just such a beast, you know? She handles everything."

TJ pulls his shirt on and gathers his stuff, looking even sexier as he gets dressed and ruffles his hair. "Well, whatever it is, Superwoman is coming in hot to get it all handled."

I pause getting ready for a minute, stepping over to him as I fold into his arms. "You flatter me."

"You deserve to be flattered." He kisses the top of my head.

"Do you need a ride home?" I ask, pulling away. "I can drop you off before I go to the office."

"No, no." He waves a hand. "Please don't worry about it. You go deal with your crisis. I'll call an Uber."

"You sure?" I walk up to him, tilting my chin up to meet his eyes.

"Positive." He kisses me one last time, long and sweet and full of...potential.

"Okay, I better run." I pull away and pick my bag up off the floor, swinging it over my shoulder as I hurry out of the bedroom. "Can you lock the door when you leave?"

"Of course."

"Bye, TJ," I say over my shoulder as I open the front door. "I had an amazing night with you."

"Ditto." He shoots me a wink. "I'll call you."

I give him one last smile and hurry out to the parking lot, sliding into my car and whipping out onto the road. As I make the short drive to the office, I don't even try to stop smiling. My heart is light and my world feels as bright as the morning sunshine.

Whatever this sudden work crisis is, I'm more than ready to deal with it.

I park my car and take the elevator up to the dingy little shoebox, still smiling like a freaking schoolgirl.

"Okay, okay. I'm here, Ci," I announce, swinging the door open and heading in. "Now what the heck is this big emergency?"

I glance around, first noticing Cici's empty chair. Then, I see her on *top* of her desk, crouching and squatting and hugging her knees.

"What on earth is going on?" I rush over, stunned and insanely confused by her terrified positions.

"There's a..." Cici looks at me with a shocking fear in the eyes of someone who could probably beat up a MMA fighter if she wanted to. "There's a bug!" She blurts out.

Her voice is riddled with so much terror, you'd think the bug in question was wielding a double barrel shotgun.

"Are you..." I raise my brows, drawing back and studying her, trying my hardest not to laugh. "Are you being serious?"

"Uh huh." She nods frantically, pointing toward the corner of the room. "He went that way."

"He?" I slides her a look, laughing as I process this. "You have got to be kidding. Cici, girl, you're fearless!" I choke on a shocked laugh, feeling an odd sense of relief that there isn't an actual work problem.

"Not when it comes to insects." She shivers, her long hair falling all around her tones and muscular shoulders. "I cannot do bugs, Lilly. Cannot. And Aubrey, Mer, and Bianca are all out on calls."

I burst out laughing at the hilariousness of the situation. "Just wait until I tell you what you pulled me away from to come here."

"I'm so sorry." She gives me big, apologetic eyes. "I just...it's like a phobia, or something. Plus, he's huge."

I nod, setting my bag down.

"And fast," She adds.

I roll my eyes and let out a sigh. It's true that I'd always been the designated bug killer throughout all of our grad school apartments. Growing up in some not-so-nice houses and apartment buildings, I guess I'm a bit more desensitized to the whole *bug* thing.

Especially considering we live in South Florida.

"It's Miami, you know. There's gonna be the occasional bug." I glance around our office resentfully. "Especially in this dingy little place."

"Not in the high rises on Brickell," Cici insists. "Where we *should* be."

"Well, I want that as much as you do, Ci. Trust me. But for now...where's the little fellow?"

"*Fellow?*" She spits out. "More like demon. He's under there." Cici points to Bianca's desk in the corner of the room. "That's where I last saw him."

I walk over to the desk and bang on it. Sure enough, a little black creature scurries out from underneath.

Cici's shriek at the very sight of the bug echoes through the little room. "Make it go away!"

I laugh. "Will you chill out?" I grab an empty coffee cup from my desk and rush over to the bug, which looks like some kind of little beetle, and trap him in the cup. "Can you hand me a piece of paper?"

Cici gives me a blank paper and I slide it underneath the cup, successfully containing Public Enemy Number One.

"I'll take him outside." I carry the cup covered with the paper toward the door and bring him downstairs to the first floor to let him out in the grass.

"Yay Lilly!" Cici cheers as I walk back into the office after returning our little visitor to his natural habitat. "My hero."

"I want an award for this," I tease.

"Why didn't you just step on it?" Cici asks.

"Because, it was just a little beetle thing. He's not harming anyone. I let him outside so he can have another chance." I lift a shoulder. "He's fine."

"That's a little too much kindness. Even for you," Cici jokes.

"Perfect timing though," I say, glancing at my phone. "I think Mer, Aubrey, and Bianca should all be coming back from their clients any minute now."

"Oh good." Cici finally gets off the desk, visibly willing herself to calm down from her brush with the beetle. "Then you can tell us all about what happened last night and this morning and how terrible I am to pull you away from it."

I smile at her. "It's okay. You were scared. I will mock you endlessly for it, but I'll always be here to handle your bug fears."

She blows me a kiss.

As if right on cue, Meredith and Bianca walk in together, chatting and laughing and appearing as if both of their accounts went well.

"Hi, girls!" They grin as they stroll in and sit down at their desks.

"You missed quite a trauma." I slide Cici a look.

"I know..." Bianca glances down at her phone. "I saw

some missed texts but I figured whatever it was got handled. What happened?"

Cici and I tell them about the bug, watching as they both laugh and shake their heads at the silliness of it all.

"You, Cici?" Meredith asks. "Really?"

"Reason number five million why we need a new office," Bianca groans.

After that, Aubrey comes in, greeting us and sitting down at her desk to start writing down notes from her meeting.

"Okay…" Meredith takes a deep breath and gathers everyone's attention. "Now that we can all relax…Lilly! Please tell us about what happened last night after you guys left Coconuts Ave."

"Please," Aubrey agrees.

"We need all the details," Cici demands.

"Okay. Now that the so-called 'emergency' is handled"—I give an eye roll and use exaggerated air quotes —"And you're all back in the office, I will tell you. It was amazing. We painted together and talked and laughed and…" I let my voice trail off.

"And?" they all demand, listening eagerly.

"And we made love," I say softly, my mind flashing with images of last night's sizzling, passionate, intimate moments that completely elevated everything in this budding relationship.

"Oh!" Cici squeals. "Get it, girl!"

"Yes, babe!" Bianca claps.

"Lilly, you must really like him." Meredith smiles, her eyes wide with interest.

"I really, really like him, you guys." I lean my head

forward and rest it in my palms, letting my mind drift off into fantasy land. "This morning he told me he's falling in love with me."

A chorus of gasps fills the air.

"Oh. My. God." Bianca's jaw falls to the floor.

"Lilly!" Meredith squeals. "That's so exciting!"

"What did you say?" Aubrey asks.

"I said I feel the same way." I shake my head and smile with disbelief at the whole situation. "Because, honestly, I do."

"This is so amazing." Cici claps her hands together. "And, by the way, we all totally loved hanging out with him, as you know."

"Yes!" Aubrey agrees. "He's a welcome addition."

Warmth fills my chest. "I just can't believe this, you guys. He's almost, like, too good to be true."

"Don't say that, Lil." Cici waves a finger at me. "You deserve the absolute best."

"We should celebrate tonight!" Bianca exclaims.

"B looking for an excuse to go out..." Meredith gives a playful eye roll. "Shocker."

"I'm down to celebrate." Aubrey shrugs. "Coconuts Ave, usual time?"

"No..." Cici cocks her head. "Let's go somewhere different."

Aubrey gives a fake gasp. "You know I hate change."

I snort. "I'm down for a switch-up. Where can we go?"

"We're celebrating." Bianca shimmies. "Let's hit that super nice place on Seabreeze Road. You know, the one with the fancy outdoor dining area. What's it called? The Emerald or something like that?"

"Oh!" I nod and hold up a finger. "I know the spot you're talking about! TJ and I walked past that place the other day. After we went to the zoo."

I recall that's right about when he ducked from seeing..."someone" that he didn't want to see and pulled me to the other side of the road. I remember seeing that particular restaurant as he started acting weird.

I kind of forgot about that instance until now. I should ask him about it.

"It looked nice?" Cici asks.

"Super nice, yeah." I shrug my shoulders. "We didn't go in, just passed by. But I think it's a bar and restaurant."

"The Emerald it is, then." Meredith smiles.

"Celebrating Lilly in Love," Bianca sings dramatically.

I roll my eyes and feel my cheeks flush with warmth, leaning back into my desk chair as I swivel around.

Lilly in Love. Doesn't have a bad ring to it.

TWENTY

TJ

I couldn't do it. I couldn't freaking do it. I couldn't bring myself to look into those heart-grabbing baby blues and say, *"I've been lying about who I am this entire time. Turns out I'm everything you hate—or, think you hate. You accidentally thought I was the gardener and I never corrected you."*

The truth is going to break her pure, wonderful, vibrant heart. And I'm the one to blame. Once she finds out, this whole thing is going to feel like it was all a sham. Fake and phony. A game.

But, to me, it was the *furthest* thing from any of that. It was the most genuine and grounded and real relationship I've ever experienced. And no matter how deeply I want that to be reality...it's not. I'm Theodore Rinehart Junior... billionaire, trust fund kid, Ivy League grad...the literal *worst* in the eyes of Lilly McCarthy.

Add liar to that resume and it's pretty much guaranteed I never see her again.

I know I have to tell her the truth. Despite the incredible, passionate, intimate, and amazing night we had together...it's not right to keep up the charade any longer. And since I clearly have absolutely no ability to tell her the truth to her face, I'm going to write it all down.

So, here I am. Staring at a blank document on my computer screen, watching the cursor flash over and over, pushing me to start typing, but, God, I don't want to.

"Okay..." I puff out on a sigh, resting my hands on the keyboard and swallowing the harsh sadness that settles in my gut.

Just tell the truth, TJ.

Lilly...

First, I want to tell you that getting to know you has been the most wonderful and eye-opening thing I've experienced in a really long time. Since the moment I met you—and accidentally drenched you in sprinkler water—the thought of you has constantly and reliably made me smile.

I feel like I was able to be my true self with you. No pretense...no expectations...just me. I haven't really felt that before, in any relationship. There's always been an agenda, a plan, a sense of...ulterior motives with the women I've dated.

But not you. You only ever saw me for me, without any of the extra stuff that comes with the truth about who I am.

So...that's what I'm getting at. I have to tell you that I'm not a gardener. You thought I was, and I thought you were adorable, so I rolled with it. At first, almost as a joke. It was endearing and cute. But then I realized how freeing it was to be with someone who didn't know who I actually am. I got carried away with the escape that it brought me. An escape from an oppressive life that I've been desperate for a break from.

Who I actually am, in that life—the real one—is...Theodore Rinehart Junior...billionaire hedge fund manager at Rinehart Investing. You never met the rich guy who owns the house because...I am the rich guy who owns the house. I know, I know. It seems like I played you. But I promise you, every feeling I had for you, every moment we shared, everything I said to you...that was all completely real. That was the realest anything has ever been for me.

I came to Florida for the winter, looking for an escape. When I met you and this whole crazy impulsive thing happened, you fit right into that escape. You gave me a chance to stop being seen as the billionaire and just be seen as TJ. I am so insanely grateful for that.

. . .

Well...that's it. That's the whole truth. And I'm gonna take a wild guess that you have absolutely no interest in seeing me or talking to me ever again, and I can't say I blame you. Not only did I keep the truth from you, turns out I'm the perfect embodiment of everything you absolutely cannot stand. Lucky me, huh?

Anyway, I've loved every second with you, and I want to make sure you know that everything I said was sincere. I really can't emphasize that enough. I had to write this all down because every time I wanted to tell you in person, I couldn't seem to get the words out. Thank you for the wonderful memories, and the chance to truly be myself.

I wish you nothing but the best, and of course I'm here if you want to talk.

TJ Rinehart

As I type my name at the bottom of the page, I lean my elbows onto my desk and let my head fall into my hands.

Dammit, why does this have to hurt so much? Why did this have to happen this way? Blake and Dominic were absolutely, painfully right. This definitely blew up in my face.

I hate that it has to end. I've never felt so much excitement for any relationship ever. She's so ridiculously special and perfect and everything I could ever want.

Maybe there's still hope. Maybe she'll see that I'm being genuine now and I'm showing all my cards and she'll throw caution to the wind and give it a shot. She is a caution-to-the-wind type of girl, after all.

Clinging to that tiny and quite possibly delusional last shred of hope, I print off the piece of paper and fold it up, heading out to my car to drive over to her place, not entirely sure what my game plan is right now.

Maybe I'll just leave it in the mailbox. Maybe I'll knock on the door and give it to her face to face.

She just has to get past the fact that everything she thought she knew about me wasn't true. That's not too much to ask, is it?

Yikes.

As I get into my car and pull out of the long, round driveway, images of that first conversation where she was standing right in this very spot flash through my mind. Her pink blouse, her little high heels. The way she carried herself with the perfect combination of confidence and humility. Her laugh, her eyes…everything.

The sun is setting as I drive down the road, the sinking disappointment of reality pressing onto my shoulders.

Should I just leave the letter and go?

I don't want to do that, but I don't know if I can stand to watch her heart break right in front of me as she realizes everything has been built on a lie.

TWENTY-ONE

LILLY

"This place is bougalicious." Bianca smiles down at her fancy pink cocktail.

I grin widely and wrap an arm around her. "It's fun, isn't it?"

"Amazing," Cici says on a content sigh as we all settle into a cozy corner booth, drinks in hand and smiles on our faces.

"Well..." Meredith lifts up her glass. "To Lilly. And her potential happily ever after."

The words send a tingle racing down my spine.

Could it be?

"How about..." I lift my martini. "To the fab five. Where would we be without each other?"

"Lost..." Aubrey shakes her head dramatically. "And hopelessly confused."

"To love," Bianca adds in, a tone of seriousness that is rare in her voice. "In all of its many forms."

"To love!" we all exclaim, clinking our glasses and laughing softly as we sip our expensive cocktails and drink in the warmth and luxury of the atmosphere.

It's dimly lit, with soft music playing and the lull of a small crowd humming through the air.

I try desperately to focus on the moment and my girls and this bar but...my mind keeps flashing back to TJ. And every flash is accompanied with a swarm of butterflies.

"Aubs, any update on the Zachary Thorne prospect?" I ask, in an attempt to get my brain to at least try to focus on something other than TJ.

"I'm going to contact the real estate agent." Aubrey raises a brow.

Bianca laughs adoringly. "Of course you are."

"He's scheduled to move in about six months from now."

"Casa De Cash, here we come," Bianca sings.

I shake my head and smile, basking in the sunny glow of that one particular moment when everything in life seems to be going just...right. "I can't believe we could actually have a client as high profile as Zachary Thorne."

"A true household name," Cici adds, sipping her drink. "Insanity."

I glance to my right, where Meredith is tense and quiet and staring intently down into her cosmopolitan.

"Mer..." I say softly. "What's wrong?"

"Nothing," she answers, quick and stern and just snappy enough to send the message that it's not a good time to pry.

Something about the mention of Zachary Thorne really

seems to get to her. Maybe it's just her Bad Boy Radar going off the freaking charts.

"So, Lil." Aubrey narrows her gaze at me. "When's the wedding?"

"Will you hush?" I shove her playfully from across the table, biting back my smile.

"When will you see him again?" Meredith asks, perking up a bit at the change of subject. "Do you at least know that far in advance?"

"Uh, I don't know." I shrug and take a small sip. "We didn't really get to plan anything because I was in such a rush when I left this morning." I glare at each of them individually. "Because my dear and slightly incompetent friend couldn't handle a little bug."

"Little? It sounded like he was more than little." Bianca snorts.

"You could have strapped a saddle on that thing and competed in the Kentucky Derby," Cici chimes in, wrinkling her nose with disgust.

As we all laugh and chat and relax in our favorite company, I let my mind slip back over and over to the fantasy that is TJ. I'm like a middle schooler with a crush.

What's he doing right now? What's he thinking about? Is he thinking about me?

I'm pathetic. And I don't even care.

I keep thinking about last night. The way everything felt so unbelievably perfect. And not just the physical stuff. Obviously, that was amazing. But the way we connected. The way I felt sexy and beautiful and loved and *seen*. It was like a breath of intoxicating fresh air.

"Hey, earth to Lilly." Bianca snaps in my face, bringing me back to reality.

"Hey, sorry I was—"

"Daydreaming about Prince Charming?" Aubrey asks with a soft chuckle. "We figured."

"Hey, that's why we're here celebrating in the first place, isn't it?" I insist, sticking my tongue out playfully. "A gal can daydream."

"We're all just jealous, truthfully," Meredith admits, lifting a shoulder.

I glance around and notice that most of their drinks are empty or almost empty. Dang...how long was I down that rabbit hole of TJ thoughts?

"I'll go grab us another round." I stand up with a smile, scooting out of the leather seat of the booth and heading over to the long bar that stretches along the back wall.

There are a couple of bartenders helping some customers, so I sit down on a stool and run my fingers along the shiny, dark wood of the bar as I wait.

I notice, out of the corner of my eye, a couple of guys sitting next to me, a few seats away at the bar. They're young, probably a little older than I am, but I can tell that they've got money. Big money. Real money. The flashy kind of money that wears a Rolex and obviously very expensive suits.

I can smell from here that they're finance guys, both cute and nice looking, but with that air of wealth and cockiness.

I have to force myself not to wrinkle my nose.

"I know, bro. I know," one of them says, swirling a glass

of beer around and laughing to the other. "His life is a mess."

"A hot mess," the other agrees, shaking his head. "I don't envy TJ one bit, that's for sure."

My heart does a tiny little kick, and I feel myself freeze, every cell in my body suddenly laser focused on their conversation.

The odds that they're talking about *my* TJ are obviously ridiculously slim. I highly doubt the sweet, humble gardener runs in the Wall Street Wannabes circles here. But...still. I can't help but listen.

"I just can't believe it," one of the guys continues, running a hand through his hair. "I really can't."

"We tried to warn him," says the other. "We tried to tell him that this entire thing was going to blow up in his face like the Fourth of July."

"I mean...dude." Finance Guy Number One chuckles and rolls his eyes. "Pretending to be a *gardener*? What on earth was he thinking?"

"It was a pretty shocking lapse in judgement, that's for sure."

Okay, now my heart is pumping. Racing, in fact, a million miles per hour. I can feel my throat tighten and my body start to go numb.

Did I actually hear that right? Did that guy just say their friend TJ...the one who is *pretending to be a gardener*?

I swallow and steady myself, praying I don't fall right off of this barstool and onto the floor.

"I almost feel bad for that girl, you know?" the one guy says, lifting a cocky shoulder. "The maid chick or whoever."

"I know. He's totally playing her."

TJ...gardener...maid chick...

Oh. My. God.

What the freaking heck is going on?

"I feel bad for her, too! She's dating a billionaire and she doesn't even know it." He sips his beer.

"TJ's an idiot for not telling her. She'd be totally locked down in two seconds if she had any idea who he was."

"Homeboy wants to play some good ole fashioned cat and mouse, I guess."

At this point, my ears are ringing and the room is spinning and I can't take it anymore. Something that feels like tears is stinging behind my eyes, and my hands are starting to shake.

Billionaire. He said that TJ is a *billionaire.*

I have to actually force myself to breathe as I attempt to even start processing what I just heard, clutching the bar with both hands for support.

Billionaire...the house...the owner...the fact that I've never met him...

It all starts to click. It's him. There is no mysterious, old stuffy rich guy who owns the mansion and is elusive and impossible to reach.

TJ is the billionaire.

And he lied to me. He's been lying to me for weeks... leading me on...playing me. Like a game of freaking cat and mouse.

The world shifts under me as I slide off of the barstool, holding myself together with the tiniest thread of sanity.

I walk back to the booth where my friends are all

sitting, and they take one look at me and instantly can tell something is wrong. "I, um..."

"Honey." Bianca stands up, placing a protective hand on my shoulder.

"Lilly." Meredith gasps. "What happened?"

"What's wrong?" Cici and Aubrey ask.

"I just...I have to go," I croak, my voice shaky.

"Lil..."

"I'll talk to you guys tomorrow. I'll explain. I just..." My throat pinches, tears threatening and anger and hurt coursing through me. "I need to go right now."

"Can I walk you home?" Meredith offers, never wavering in her sweetness.

"No, no. I'm okay." I swallow and take a deep breath. "It's right up the road. I'm fine. I just want to go home."

Before they have a chance to protest and insist someone comes with me, I pivot and head out of the restaurant, pulling shallow, quivering breaths in as I walk.

The walk home is a blur. My mind is racing and swirling and jumping around.

He lied. He faked who he was. He pretended to be something he wasn't for the entire time I've known him. The whole relationship was built on...a lie. On phoniness. On a fake persona because he couldn't be man enough to show me the real him.

My heart aches and my body is tired and hurt. Tears fall down my cheeks as I head down the sidewalk as fast as I can, desperate to get home and curl up and somehow attempt to even begin to deal with this.

I got played. I got fooled. I fell for a complete and total liar, and believed every word he told me.

I finally can see my building, and I'm out of breath from speed walking as I reach it. The world melts and swims behind my tears, and I wipe them furiously, unable to decide between sadness and anger.

I head through the parking lot, feeling my chest shake with the first of probably many sobs.

God, I just want to be home. I just freaking want to be home, and I never want to see his stupid, fake, lying face again.

I stomp toward the stairs and down the hallway, stopping in complete and total shock as I get closer to my front door.

It's him. Unless I'm completely hallucinating...TJ the Lying Billionaire is sitting on my doorstep.

I gasp as emotion racks me, my jaw clenched and my chest tight.

"Lilly." He stands up eagerly as soon as he sees me coming, those familiar brown eyes dumping pounds of salt into my fresh and confused wound.

I exhale sharply, squeezing my eyes shut.

"Lilly, I need to tell you something. I—"

"Save it," I cut him off, avoiding eye contact as much as I can. "I already know."

"You what?" He draws back.

"I already know that you're a complete liar and you used me and you manipulated me and...I found it all out from your little Ivy League friends at the bar."

"From...*who*?" He furrows his brow in confusion, his expression riddled with panic as he starts piecing it together. "Oh. Oh, God. Crap."

"Yeah. Crap is right," I say sternly.

"Lilly, please just listen to me."

"Is it true that you're a billionaire and you've been lying to me this entire time pretending to be a gardener?" I ask, not even caring about the tear that drips down my cheek.

"Well...yes, but—"

"Then I have nothing left to say to you."

TWENTY-TWO

TJ

"I know how it looks, and I know it seems like I lied, but you have to understand—"

"Understand what?" She whips her head around, her eyes rimmed in red from crying and her cheeks pink.

The sight makes my heart hurt and gets me even more pissed at myself and filled with regret.

"That I...it wasn't planned," I insist desperately, knowing there's really no possible way I can save this at this point. "None of it was planned. It just sort of...happened."

"So you just..." She frowns as the corners of her mouth turn down. "Decided on the fly that you were gonna use me to...to...prove some stupid point?" She practically spits the word out.

"What? No. Prove what point?"

"I don't know!" She throws her hands up, frustrated and visibly hurt. "It seems like you wanted to prove that you could get a girl to fall for you, even when she didn't know about your billions of dollars. When she thought you were a gardener." She narrows her gaze, those blue eyes stabbing me.

"It was nothing like that," I insist.

"How was it nothing like that?" Her brows knit together in sadness, and confusion and frustration are written all over her face. "That's exactly what it was. You wanting to play...*cat and mouse*, I believe was the terminology."

"Huh?" I angle my head.

Now *I'm* the one who's frustrated and confused.

"It was never a game," I say, purposely keeping my tone as steady as I can, desperately wishing she would trust me.

But why would she? Who can blame her?

"What, was it just too easy for you when you flashed your dollars?" Her voice breaks with hurt, gutting me. "You wanted a challenge?"

"No." I shake my head, wishing so badly I could just touch her and hold her and make her understand how I feel. "It was nothing even close to that, Lilly."

I level my eyes on hers, wishing I had better answers. Wishing there was a way for her to understand how genuine everything between us actually was.

I tuck the folded letter into my back pocket. As soon as I got here, I realized I needed to man up and tell her face to face, so I waited on the doorstep for her to come home. And before I could even try to explain...she found out in the absolute worst imaginable way.

She lets out a deep breath, shutting her eyes and pinching the bridge of her nose. "I hate dishonesty. And you're deep in a freaking pool of it."

I swallow, the truth of that statement stabbing me. "I know."

"I just..." Her voice breaks again. "I think you should go."

Disappointment crashes over me, and every fiber of my body wants nothing more than to stay. To try and explain. To...hope.

But I can tell from the pain and betrayal written all over her face...there is no hope left.

"Okay," I say, sliding the folded-up piece of paper out of my pocket and handing it to her. "Here, take this."

"What is this?"

"I came here to drop this off, but then I decided to stay and tell you in person. It's a letter, and it explains what happened, and why it happened, and how I feel."

She glares at me, her eyes darkening as they meet mine. "What about how I feel, TJ?" She scoffs. "Is that even your name?"

"Theodore Junior," I say softly. "Yes."

"Right." She rolls her eyes and gives a dry, sarcastic laugh. "Of course."

"Just...read it if you want to." I turn and walk away from her, feeling my body and heart and mind pulling me like a magnet in the opposite direction.

I desperately want to hear her call my name or say something or stop me, but all I hear is her front door open and slam shut.

TWENTY-THREE

LILLY

"I'm just...I'm having a really hard time processing this." Meredith shakes her head, curling up in the corner of my sofa and giving me a sweetly sympathetic look.

"Yeah. You and me both." I sniff, hugging my knees to my chest.

"It's just..." Bianca paces around the living room, her mouth wide open with shock. "It's disgusting, is what it is."

Aubrey and Cici just stare at me, as stunned and confused as I was when I first found out the truth.

After he left and I calmed down a bit, I called my girls for support. Of course they were over here in record time to surround me with a sea of shoulders to cry on.

I'm still comprehending everything, and desperately wishing that it was all just some stupid mistake...that he wasn't the TJ those guys were talking about. But as soon as

I saw his face standing outside my door—I knew it was all true.

"You think he was planning on telling you?" Aubrey asks, handing me a cup of tea that I didn't even notice her make.

"He claims that's why he was here, to finally come clean." I rub my eyes. "He gave me a letter that he'd brought with him, but I...don't really feel like reading it right now. I can't take any more of this."

"So he's the billionaire." Aubrey shakes her head in shock, sitting back down next to me on the sofa. "It was him the whole time."

"Did you have any clue?" Cici asks, leaning forward to look at me. "I mean, did you have any idea that there was *something* up?"

"Yeah..." I sip the hot tea and let the steam rise around my face. "I guess there were some moments when I felt like he was definitely holding back. But, you know, I just figured it's a new relationship and he has some walls up and..." I shrug. "I never thought he was being completely fake."

"He must be a good actor." Bianca clicks her tongue.

"What I don't get is...why?" Meredith angles her head, frowning with confusion. "Why not tell you the truth?"

"Yeah." Aubrey laughs dryly. "Billions of dollars aren't exactly a huge turn-off."

"No kidding," Bianca agrees.

"I don't know." I wrap my hands around the hot mug and hold it close to my chest. "I guess it was some sort of game to him."

"God, Lil." Meredith leans against me. "I'm so sorry."

"I never saw this coming." Bianca sits down on the floor, slumping over. "He seemed so...genuine. So real."

"You're telling me," I say under my breath.

"Wait...I have a question." Aubrey holds up a finger, narrowing her gaze as if she's suddenly deep in thought.

"Ask away." I wave a hand. "I, unlike some people, am an open book."

Mer squeezes my arm.

"When you met him that first day, outside the big house. You were there for a consultation, right?"

"Yeah." I nod.

"And when you couldn't find Theodore," Aubrey continues slowly, "who you assumed was some old, stuffy, gray-haired rich guy, you wandered around the property a bit and ran into..."

"TJ," I finish, not sure where this is going.

"So, when you first saw TJ, did he introduce himself as the gardener? Like he just outright lied? Or did you assume he was the gardener based on what he was doing, and he just never corrected you?"

I lean back against the couch cushions, letting out a deep sigh. "I made the assumption. It was a mistake, obviously, that could have been so easily corrected. He was back in the bushes messing with a sprinkler. He was wearing a dirty T-shirt and was covered in sweat. He didn't exactly look like your textbook hedge fund manager." I try not to cry at the memory. "So I was like, hey. You must be the gardener. And he smiled and...didn't say otherwise."

"So it wasn't some sort of elaborate scheme then, is what you're saying, Aubs," Meredith clarifies.

"Right." Aubrey nods. "It was almost like he just decided to go with it on the fly."

"But that doesn't answer the question of...why." Cici shakes her head, her black bangs dancing around her forehead.

"I can't sit here and dig for answers, you guys." I run a hand through my tangled mess of hair. "I got played. He saw the opportunity when I made that silly but understandable mistake of his identity. And he used me as some sort of fun little game."

"Oh, Lil." Aubrey squeezes onto the couch with the rest of us and wraps her arms around me. "It's not fair."

"It's life." I shut my eyes.

"I don't know, Lilly." Bianca lifts a shoulder and widens her gaze. "Maybe you should...hear him out. At least have a conversation. Maybe."

I look up at her, my lashes still wet with tears. "Uh, no."

"Why not? That's the least he owes you. And besides, what if it wasn't all fake? What if it wasn't all a game? I just have to believe you guys had something real."

The words make my heart kick. It felt real. Every second of it felt amazingly, genuinely real.

"It was all based on a lie," I say, my voice steady and flat. "There's nothing more to say."

"I don't know, Lil." Meredith glances at me.

I turn to her, tilting my head with surprise. "What do you mean?"

"B might have a point. What if there's actually a really good explanation for all this?"

"What if it's all explained in the letter?" Cici chimes in, flicking her brows.

"No." I wrinkle my nose and shake my head quickly, taking another warm sip of herbal tea. "A lie is a lie. Besides, I heard his stupid, entitled friends. They literally were joking about him playing a game of cat and mouse and messing with some 'poor maid girl.'"

Meredith cringes. "Yikes."

"Yeah," I snort sarcastically. "Yikes is right."

"So the friends are jerks." Bianca shrugs. "And maybe he is, too. Probably. But you don't know the whole story, yet."

"I know enough," I say, sadness tugging at my heart and weighing me down. "I know enough to be sure that someone who is this dishonest and fake isn't someone I want to be with."

"I get that. I really do." Aubrey nods slowly. "The risk of getting hurt is just too high."

"I already got hurt," I say, a sob threatening to break in my throat.

As we sit and talk and think and cry, wrapped up in throw blankets and lying on cushions, the hours start to fall away. I feel calmer and more okay, but the normal hope and optimism and excitement that usually drive me are entirely gone, replaced by gloomy, empty heartbreak.

TWENTY-FOUR

TJ

I watch the stupid clock on my wall ticking away one second at a time. Glancing out of the front window of my home office, I stare at the driveway, flooded with memories and images of Lilly. The way she would hop out of the Maid In Miami van in her pink shirt and white sneakers with that ponytail swinging around. The way I'd be so freaking excited to see her, just to be around her.

Images of her soaked by the sprinkler, laughing wildly and probably thinking I'm the worst gardener on the face of the earth.

I grit my teeth and let another wave of regret wash over me. I should have just come clean. Right there, right in that moment. I should have just said, "Oh no, I'm not the gardener. I'm Theodore, the owner of this house. Nice to meet you."

But...I don't know. If I had done that, if I had just corrected her at first...none of it would have happened. I would have been her boss, and she would have curled her lip at my upbringing and privilege. We'd have been attracted to each other, sure, but there could have never been the blissful freedom that I found in our relationship.

I never would have gotten the chance to fall in love, and be loved back, for exactly who I am.

God, I wish she had just been able to read the freaking letter before finding everything out. But, realistically, I don't think it would really have changed anything. Dishonesty is dishonesty, and there's no coming back.

The reality of that stabs my gut, hard.

I run my hands through my hair, not physically able to stand sitting at this desk staring at the clock and the computer screen for another second.

I pull out my phone and text my pilot, telling him to have my jet ready to take me back to New York City first thing tomorrow morning. As much as it hurts, as much as it completely sucks...I've got to get out of here. My relaxing escape from reality turned into, well, heartbreak. And I really don't have anyone to blame but myself.

Restless and unfocused, I stand up and walk out of the office and down the hall, heading out through the sliding glass doors onto the back patio. The sky is cloudy and gray, threatening a nasty storm that feels just perfectly appropriate for my mood right now.

I walk around the pool, feeling a confusing mixture of emotions about this house and this place and this city. For a short, quick, fleeting moment...I was the happiest I've ever been here. But I wasn't me. I was living a lie.

I pull out my phone and stare at the screen, my fingers

deciding to have a mind of their own. Before I have a chance to give it any thought, I'm calling my father.

My insanely hardworking, brilliant, intimidating but loving dad who raised me by himself from nine years old on, and would do absolutely anything for me. The man loves work, no doubt about that, but he's always been there for every aspect of my life. As messy and bizarre as this situation is, I know he'll be there. And frankly, I need him.

"TJ!" he exclaims as he answers the call, his voice booming and deep. "How's it going? Did you end up hiring those new associates?"

"Yeah, Dad, hey. I'm not..." I run a hand through my hair and glance up at the storm clouds. "I'm not actually calling about work."

"It's three PM on a Thursday, what the heck else are you doing?" he teases, the sarcasm in his voice making me relax.

I force a soft laugh.

"What's up, kid?" The familiar warmth of my dad's voice instantly makes me feel like calling him was the right choice.

"I kind of got myself into this...weird situation."

"And this isn't work related?" he clarifies.

"No, no. It's...personal. It involves a woman."

"Ah." I can practically hear my dad nodding and wagging a finger at me. "I should have guessed. Hit me with your weird situation, then. I got time."

As I explain the details of my relationship with Lilly... the mistake, the lie, the way she found out, the letter...my dad listens, asks a couple of questions, and takes it all in. I hear how ridiculous it sounds, but he doesn't make me feel ridiculous at all, which is reassuring.

"So...that's basically it. As far as I can tell, she never wants to see me or talk to me again." I let out a breath after rambling on for God knows how long.

"Wow. That's uh..." He chuckles. "That certainly is a unique predicament you're in, son."

"Yeah...I know."

"Well, what are you going to do?" he asks, eagerness hinting in his tone.

"What's left for me to do?" I run a hand through my hair and continue walking circles around the pool, feeling the first couple of raindrops fall onto my forehead. "I texted Pete. I'm packing up tonight and he's flying me back to New York tomorrow morning. There's nothing more I can do."

The reality of going back to Manhattan tomorrow makes my stomach tighten. Nothing sounds worse, but what else can I do?

"Now why in the world are you doing that?" my dad asks.

I stop pacing for a second, surprised by his response. "What do you mean?" I laugh softly. "It's the only thing to do. Things with Lilly and me are over. She hates me. I've got to get back to New York and my real life."

"TJ...that is definitely not what you need to do," Dad says sternly, using his business voice.

"What? Of course it is. I'm not going to stay here, there's no reason to—"

"Listen, son." He takes a deep breath, the telltale sign that he's gearing up to say something profound. "It sounds like you found someone who you really, deeply care about."

"Well, yeah. I did. She's amazing. But there's no way she would ever—"

"And..." he cuts me off. "I'm going to give you a piece of advice. As we all know, I'm by no means the king of lasting relationships."

A pang hits my heart at the thought of my mom leaving.

"I still want your advice," I say gently.

"Good. Because I'm giving it either way." I can hear him smile. "I've lived without a romantic partner for the last sixteen years. I raised you on my own, and we had a dang good time, didn't we?"

I chuckle. "Heck yeah, we did."

"But...I was alone. I was without a wife, without a partner. I never found that special magical feeling again. Probably because your mother scarred me and ruined me for women everywhere. But...that doesn't have to happen to you, TJ. You deserve to have what I never did. It's rare and it's fleeting and it's really hard to come by."

"Thanks, Dad. I really appreciate that. But..." I pinch the bridge of my nose and sit down on a patio chair. "As much as I want to be with Lilly, I'm telling you there's no chance she wants anything to do with me."

"You said you felt like what you had with her was real, yes?"

"Completely real," I say with certainty. "It was the most true to myself I've ever been, ironically enough."

"She didn't know about the money, so she got to know you without it. It didn't play a role," he clarifies and justifies my feelings, like he truly understands.

"Yes! Exactly."

"And you think she's really the one for you?"

"I think she could have been. If...you know...the circumstances were entirely different."

"TJ..." My dad clears his throat. "Don't give up. Don't fly back to New York. Not yet, anyway."

"Dad...I don't have a choice. It's over."

"It might be. But you can't give up," he insists. "I'm not going to let you just walk away from something like this, when I personally know how special and rare it is. You've got to just go all in. Leave everything you've got on the table."

"Like...a big move?"

"A big move," he says, excitement rising in his voice and, admittedly, transferring a bit over to me. "And if she says no and tells you to screw off? Then, you lost. And you come back to Manhattan and pick up the pieces. But if she says yes...you'll be glad you listened to your old man."

I stand up and start pacing again, a new zing of hope and possibility zipping down my spine. "Huh...I guess it doesn't hurt to throw one last-ditch effort out."

"It's like we always say at the firm...high risk, high reward."

"But, Dad, you always want to minimize risks." I give an easy laugh, the wheels of my brain turning at high speed.

"But you don't," he says, matter of fact. "Is she worth it?"

"Yes," I say with zero hesitation. "Without a doubt."

"Cancel the jet, son. Make your big move."

"Okay..." I take a deep breath and head back into the house as the rain starts picking up. "You're right."

"Of course I am. That's why you called me."

"Thanks, Dad."

He's right. I'm not ready to give up. I'm not going to let this slip away without at least one last attempt to get her back. She's more than worth it.

I just have to come up with a way to show her how sincere I am, and it's gotta be...big.

TWENTY-FIVE

LILLY

SUDDENLY, MY PHONE VIBRATES FROM INSIDE MY purse, which is laying on the ground next to my desk.

"Who's texting you?" Meredith asks, her gaze wide with curiosity. "Could it be...?"

"I think there's just about one person who that could be," Cici whispers, nodding toward my purse.

I haven't looked at the phone in hours—not since we got back from lunch—and I've tried desperately to immerse myself in work and forget about the whole TJ thing. I've been...not very successful. But I'm trying.

But now my heart starts to pump at the thought of a text from him, even though I don't want it. I don't want to see his stupid, lying name on that screen.

Except...I do. A little bit. Because feelings don't just disappear in a couple days, no matter how badly you want them to.

"Should I check it?" I ask.

"Um, yes!" Bianca urges.

"Oh, I just know that boy is absolutely drowning in regret right now," Cici asserts. "Drowning."

"Of course he is," Meredith agrees. "He just lost the best damn girl he'll ever meet."

Bianca laughs softly and slides Mer a look. "Did you just say damn? I think that's the closest you've ever come to cursing."

She folds her arms and straightens her back. "I can't help it. I lose all control when somebody wrongs one of my friends."

This makes me smile as nerves jitter through me on the topic of the phone. It only buzzed once, the way it does when I receive a text.

"You guys really think it's him? It's probably my mom or something." I wave a dismissive hand.

"I know for a fact that Shirley McCarthy is in Vermont. With Bill." Bianca arches a brow and points at my bag on the ground.

I laugh and slide her a look. "How do you know more about my parents' vacations than I do?"

"I follow their travel blog. Duh. And the only other people who would text you at this hour are all sitting in this tiny shoebox of an office. Now go read it, would you?"

"She's right," Aubrey agrees.

"Okay, okay." I take a deep breath and lean down to grab my purse, plopping it into my lap. I dig out the phone and turn it over to see the screen.

TJ: *1 New Message*

I gasp a little, surprised even though I had a gut feeling

they were right about it being TJ. "It's him," I say quickly, looking back at all of them.

"Read, girl!" Meredith urges.

After one more deep breath, I click on the message and let my eyes skim through it before reading it out loud.

"Lilly. I am so, insanely sorry for everything that happened, and I can't stand how badly I hurt you."

"Aw," Meredith interjects.

"No aww's!" I demand, glaring at her.

"Is there more?" Aubrey presses.

"Yeah, I'll keep going." I look back down at the text and read from where I left off. "I completely get it if you hate me and never want to speak to me again, but I would really give anything for one last shot with you. I can't give up what we had without a fight. If you have even the littlest desire to see me, meet me at 1804 Brickell Ave, upstairs in Suite 1760 tonight at 6PM. If you don't come, I'll take no as your answer and leave you alone."

I draw in a slow, shaky breath as I try to process what I just read. "I'm not going," I say softly, flipping the phone over and setting it face down on my desk.

"What?" Bianca gasps. "What do you mean you're not going?"

"Clearly this guy is all in for you, Lil." Cici raises her brows and leans forward, searching my face. "Don't you want to give it a chance?"

"I gave it a chance, you guys." I throw my hands up, too overwhelmed with emotion to even think straight. "I was all in. I was one hundred percent ready to dive in with him and give it everything I had. He lied to me. And not just some petty, little lie. He literally was wearing an entirely fake identity for our whole relationship. How could you possibly be thinking I should give him another chance?" I swallow, my voice desperate with emotion and frustration and the rawness of the hurt.

"Lilly..." Meredith draws out my name, soft and sweet as usual. "Don't you want to at least hear his explanation?"

"I don't see how there could possibly by a good explanation for this, Mer." I take a deep breath and steady myself, shaking my head as I continue trying to comprehend what I just read and the cocktail of feelings that go along with it.

"Isn't it worth just hearing him out, though?" Cici asks.

I turn to Aubrey, who is my go-to when I need practicality and risk management. "Aubs? You think it'd be stupid and crazy to go, right?"

She shrugs. "It's up to you, hun. I just...I don't want to see you get any more hurt than you already are. But..."

"But?" I demand.

"It may be worth a shot. I don't know."

I groan loudly and rock back in my chair, grabbing fistfuls of hair. "Why did this all have to be such a mess?"

I think for a few minutes, swiveling around in my desk chair.

"It's after five..." Meredith points out.

"I'm gonna head home," I say, my body tense and my jaw tight.

"Lil..." Bianca starts.

"I just..." I hold up my hand and shake my head. "My mind is made up. He faked everything and there is nothing he could say or do that's gonna change that. Can you guys lock up here? I want to go home."

"Of course," Meredith says kindly.

"Take care of yourself, Lil." Cici stands up from her desk to give me a hug as I grab my purse and laptop and get ready to leave.

I give hugs to all four of them, wishing this storm cloud of sadness could somehow magically be lifted. But it can't, and it won't. Right now, I just have to be sad.

But I'm not going to meet him at...some random location. He was fake with me, and I only found out the real truth because I overheard some guys talking in a bar.

The reality of that stings all over again.

"Bye, guys." I wave weakly as I leave the office and head down the hallway, doubt pressing down on my shoulders.

When I finally get into my car, I drop my forehead onto the steering wheel and squeeze my eyes shut, thinking about that text.

And then, I remember that I wadded up his letter, having never read it, and shoved it in my glovebox so I wouldn't dwell.

I swallow hard and take a deep breath, sitting in the parking lot, shaky and uncertain and sad. I reach over into the glove compartment and pull out the folded paper, a tear threatening as I open it up and start to read.

My eyes slowly take in every word, my heart pulling and tugging with how poignantly sincere he sounds. This is...him. This is the TJ I fell in love with. He's real, but he's...not real.

I keep reading one sentence at a time, emotion rising as the words flow through my head.

But I promise you, every feeling I had for you, every

moment we shared, everything I said to you...that was all completely real. That was the realest anything has ever been for me.

Does he...mean that?

"No," I say out loud to myself. "No, no, no. I'm not falling for this crap. I'm not letting him play me again." I grit my teeth, willing myself to stay strong and tough and say *screw him.*

But...these words feel genuine. They feel as genuine as everything he said to me. What if he really does mean them? What if he's not just some jerk billionaire who wanted to play games?

I guess there's only one way to find out.

I whip out of the parking lot and start heading down the road, setting my GPS to direct me to 1804 Brickell Ave.

———

My heart slams in my chest as I walk into the lobby of the building, icy cold air conditioning adding to the chills that are already spreading across my skin.

I don't know what to think or feel or expect, and the anticipation of the unknown is giving me jitters.

It's an office building—a dang nice one—reaching forty stories high in the most beautiful part of Miami's business district. It's clean and sleek and everything feels high-end. I imagine a lot of money is made in this building.

But work is about the last thing on my mind as I head to the elevator which has a directory on the wall next to it.

Where the heck am I going, and why would he want to meet me here to talk? Something is definitely up, but after reading the letter...I can't help but give in to the appeal of having just one more conversation.

There's a tiny voice nagging in the back of my mind... maybe this could be fixed.

It's doubtful, it's unlikely, and it's probably incredibly stupid for me to even be here right now. But that letter felt...real. And I couldn't just let it go. And here I am.

I click the elevator button and hold my breath as one dings and the doors open, my mind racing a mile a minute with thoughts and possibilities and confusion.

What in the world am I about to walk into?

I click the button for floor 17, my palms sweaty and my body quivering a little bit.

The elevator slows to a stop and I get out, glancing around at the entrance to a long hallway, lined with doors marked for individual office suites.

Maybe this is...where he works? But why would he want me to come here? Also, I didn't see any signs for Rinehart Investing, and I'd imagine that billionaires are the type of people to want their name on a sign.

I walk down the hall slowly, glancing at each door until I finally reach Suite 1760. I check my phone...it's 6:02. Fashionably late, I guess.

My heart is pumping rapidly now, adrenaline flooding my veins.

I'm still mad at him, and seriously hurt by him, but I know I can't completely let this whole thing go without one final answer.

With a deep breath and a silent beg for confidence, I yank the door open and enter Suite 1760.

I'm instantly struck by a flood of natural light filling a

huge, open space with clean gray wooden floors and floor-to-ceiling windows. It's stunning—light and bright and airy and gleaming with luxury.

I suck in a breath of air as I look around, completely puzzled.

"Hi." A voice—his voice—breaks through the silence and startles me.

I look over to see TJ walking from around the corner of the huge, empty office space. He's wearing a white T-shirt and faded jeans, looking at me as if he's shocked I'm actually here.

Honestly, *I'm* shocked I'm actually here.

"You came," he says, his eyes wide and bright and filled with a thousand emotions.

"Yeah, I..." I look around the office, shrugging and gesturing. "What in the world is this place? Why did you ask me to meet you here? You know, if you wanted to talk, we could have just—"

"Well, first of all..." TJ steps closer to me, filling my nose with his familiar scent and almost making me momentarily forget that he's a fake phony liar gameplayer. Almost. "If I had asked you to see me just to talk, you would have said no."

"That's not true." I cross my arms and step back. "I came here, didn't I?"

"Because you were curious." He arches a brow. "No?"

"Maybe," I mutter.

"And secondly...I asked you to meet me here, because this is the new office of Maid In Miami."

My heart drops into my stomach and I feel the earth shifting underneath my feet. "It's...the...the *what*?"

"I bought it for you," TJ says, his smile sweet and kind and as sincere as he was. Or I thought he was. "And, I'm not trying to buy your forgiveness or anything like that, and if you still completely hate me, I understand. But I wanted you to have this. I wanted to show you how genuine my feelings are for you. How I never said anything to you that I didn't completely mean from the bottom of my heart. I couldn't give up on you without a fight, Lilly."

"I..." I feel my body quivering as I step around slowly, still trying not to pass out from the total shock. "I don't even know what to say." A sudden smile pulls at my cheeks as a couple of unexpected tears spring from my eyes. "You bought this for us?"

"You guys have an absolutely killer business, and you deserve the office of your dreams." TJ smiles, holding my gaze so intently and passionately it's really starting to make me forget how mad I am. "Did you...did you read the letter?"

"Yes..." I say, finally feeling somewhat stable on my feet. "That's sort of what got me here."

"Lilly." He levels his gaze with mine, placing a strong but gentle hand on my shoulder. "I meant every single word. None of this was planned or intended or calculated, and I can promise you that it was *never* a game."

"But...but why didn't you just tell me the truth?"

"Because of everything I said in the letter. Because I've never been able to be seen or loved or understood as anything but a billionaire. I finally got to just be me. You loved me without knowing about the money, and it was the most addictive and refreshing thing in the world."

"Of course I did," I whisper, my voice breaking as I

inch closer to him. "You're amazing. I just...I just wish you hadn't lied."

"I didn't lie, really. I just never corrected you. And I should have. I know I should have. But, Lilly McCarthy...I love you. And I know that you love me, too. Whether I'm a billionaire or a really crappy gardener..."

I give a tearful laugh.

"I know you love me because you got to know the real me. I was comfortable and open and myself with you in ways I've never been with anyone."

My heart tugs and pulls and everything mixes and shifts around in my head. I look around the office, my jaw still on the floor from the gesture. "Is this...this is really ours?"

"Yes." He pulls me close and smiles. "And I am so, so, so unbelievably sorry. I will never keep anything from you again if you give me another chance, I promise."

I take in a slow breath, every cell in my body screaming at me to jump into his arms so we can ride off into the sunset.

But...it happened. He lied. Well, sort of. He faked something. But his honesty now...it feels understandable. I kind of get it. And in a weird way, I'm kind of glad. Because I never would have gotten to know him or gotten involved at all if I'd known who he really was.

And maybe that's why he did it. And maybe it's good that he did.

"Hang on, before you say anything." He holds up a finger, his brown eyes dancing with an endearing kind of hope.

"There's more?" I exclaim, choking on something

between a laugh and a cry. "I don't know how much more I can handle, I..." I run my fingers along the sleek glass of the office windows, studying the gorgeous space.

I can't believe he did this for me. To show me he means it.

It wasn't a game.

"I made you something." TJ emerges from around the corner of a back hallway, carrying a big, rectangular canvas in his hands. It's angled backwards so I can't see what's on it.

"What?" I tilt my head and walk up to him. "You painted something?"

"Yeah." He glances down, lifting a humble shoulder. "It's, uh, it's silly but...I don't know. I thought it would be nice to have something personal to put on the wall of your new office."

At this point I'm warm with joy and overwhelmed with the shocking and blindsiding way this all unfolded.

"Let me see," I say excitedly.

He flips around the long canvas, holding it up in front of him.

I gasp and step back, my hand flying to my mouth as I study the canvas.

"It's..." My voice cracks with emotion. "It's us."

The canvas shows five girls...painted in an abstract, cartoon kind of way, with all different colors. In a row, there's me, Meredith, Bianca, Aubrey, and Cici. I can tell who is who from the hair and the outfits, and the whole background is decorated with bright and fun colors and patterns.

It's bursting with life and happiness, each of us in a

different pose...laughing and talking to each other with flowing dresses and long hair and animated designs. We're linking arms and holding hands and the entire energy emanating from the canvas is palpable.

"TJ..." I let a tear fall as I move my gaze to meet his. "This is incredible. And wow. You can freaking paint!"

"I was inspired." He leans the canvas against the wall behind him and steps close to me, his chest rising and falling. "By you."

"It's...spectacular. It's the most wonderful thing anyone has ever done for me," I admit, happiness bursting through me.

"Can you forgive me? Can we...start over?" He cocks his head, a hopeful smile pulling at his mouth.

Considering I've never felt as loved and adored as I do right now, I think there's an obvious answer.

"Yes," I say, letting myself fall into his arms and melt into the bliss of the moment. "But no more secrets."

"Never again." He pulls back and looks at me seriously, and I know that I trust him with my whole heart.

"I love you." I stand on my toes and plant a kiss on his lips, feeling like I could float away on a cloud of joy if I really wanted to.

"I love you, too." He squeezes his arms around me and kisses me back.

"Well, now you're dating a billionaire, and you're actually aware of it," he teases, spinning me around as I giggle wildly. "I was never anything but myself with you."

"I know." I look into his eyes, feeling happier and more hopeful than ever before. "You'd be the man of my dreams without a penny in your pocket, Theodore Rinehart."

TWENTY-SIX

TJ
Six Months Later

"So...WAS IT EVERYTHING YOU THOUGHT IT WOULD BE?"
I wrap my arm tightly around Lilly, pulling her into me as
we walk out of our luxury resort lodge, the cool air of
Alaska settling onto my skin.

"This place? It's freaking amazing! I can't believe I
finally got to come here. I'm so glad it was with you." She
takes a deep breath and shuts her eyes, drinking in the vacation of her dreams.

Or, at least, I hope it's been the vacation of her dreams.

I subtly graze my hand over my pocket to make sure the
little box is still in there, knowing this vacation is about to
get a whole lot dreamier.

"I think the spot we're going to is...just up the road
here."

"To see the Northern Lights?" she exclaims, practically
bouncing on her toes.

I don't think she has any clue that I'm going to pop the question underneath the magic of the Northern Lights, but she's already about as excited as she could possibly be.

"It's so close to us," Lilly remarks.

"I know," I thread my fingers through hers, a jitter of nervous excitement zinging through my body. "That's why I wanted to stay in this lodge tonight, in Fairbanks. Apparently, up on this hill is one of the clearest shots of the sky when the lights come."

"Wow. So that's why we left Anchorage this morning and headed over to the middle of nowhere." She turns to me, her eyes glimmering with joy. "You know I love you, right?"

I lean over and plant a kiss on her forehead. "I never would have guessed."

As we step out onto the hill, views of vast, icy mountains line the entire field of vision, with only starlight glistening down on everything around us.

It's cold and hugely open, and we're basically alone in this particular spot.

"Lilly." I take her chin in my hand and tilt it up slowly toward the night sky. "Look."

Swirls of colors dance across the dark sky, vibrant shades of neon green and purple and pink. The streaks of luminescent color echo everywhere above us, reflecting onto the snow and ice and casting everything in a glowing, radiant beam.

"Oh...my...gosh..." Lilly stares up, completely mesmerized by the beauty of it.

"Wow..." I agree, drawing back with bewilderment, so stunned by the insane natural phenomenon that I momentarily forget about the ring in my pocket and my secret agenda for the night.

"TJ...it's..." She holds her hand to her mouth, giving a soft gasp. "It's so beautiful."

"It's..." I take my gaze off of the dancing colors in the sky and let it fall down onto her. "The most beautiful thing I've ever seen."

And she is. She's brightened up my life more than these prisms in the night. Every day with Lilly has been an absolute dream come true, and I've never felt more like myself. I have absolutely zero doubts that she is the one. The only one. Forever.

I just hope she feels the same.

"They look exactly like the time I painted that canvas..." Lilly laughs softly, leaning her head onto my shoulder without peeling her eyes from the sky.

I smile warmly at the memory, shaking my head. "Only missing the orange blob."

"Oh, God. Not the orange blob."

We stand together a little longer, wrapped up in coats and completely enchanted by the beauty of this sight.

"I told you," Lilly whispers after some time. "I told you it would be amazing."

"It's exceeded my expectations for sure."

"I think this is the happiest and best and most perfect moment of my entire life." She turns to me and smiles, her face radiant and glowing as it reflects the Northern Lights.

I draw in a slow, deep breath, holding her gaze and losing myself in the blue eyes that have come to feel like home.

The best home I've ever known.

"I think I can make it even better," I say softly, inching closer to her as her eyes widen and she angles her head with curiosity.

Lilly gives a dry laugh. "How?"

I wet my lips and smile at her one more time, before dropping my knee to the ground and keeping my eyes locked on hers.

A stunned gasp slips from her throat as she jumps backwards, clearly completely floored by the fact that this is actually about to happen right now.

And...so am I. But it's so, so, obviously...right. It's perfect.

"Lilly..." I say her name, unable to contain the nervous and almost giddy smile yanking at my cheeks.

"Are you..." Her voice quivers as she chokes on a gasping laugh. "Is this..."

"You're the love of my life," I say, swallowing to gather myself—and taking in a moment that I know I will remember forever. "From the day I met you, you've shown me what real love is. What vulnerability feels like. What happiness feels like. And most of all, you've shown me the absolute best parts of myself. The version of me that I want to be forever. I can't go another day without this being completely official."

"TJ..." She croaks out my name, her shaking hands glued to her mouth.

I reach into my pocket and pull out the ring box, watching the luminescent colors dance across her eyes.

"Lilly McCarthy...will you marry me? And make me the happiest man in the entire world?"

"Yes!" she shrieks, dropping to the ground before I have a chance to stand back up.

Lilly collapses into me, folding herself against me as we hug and kiss and laugh on the crunchy, snowy ground.

Joy and elation and just the tiniest bit of relief flood me all at once, and I pull out the ring and slide it onto her finger.

"This feels like a dream," she says through a happy cry, wrapping up in my arms as we sit together and look up at the sky.

"You feel like a dream," I say, holding her close. "That's why I'm so sure about this."

"And holy cow!" She lifts up her left hand, admiring the diamond as she waves it around and makes it sparkle in the colorful light. "You weren't messing around with this thing, were you?"

I shoot her a playful wink.

"You must get paid well as the gardener," she teases, pressing her lips to mine as we laugh together.

"Very funny." I roll my eyes and kiss her over and over again.

The little mistake turned into a big secret. And the big secret turned into almost losing the best thing that ever happened to me.

Almost.

But I didn't lose her. She's right here, and she's mine, and I am never letting her go.

TWENTY-SEVEN

LILLY

"We all totally knew, by the way," Bianca asserts, sipping her latte as we gather in the huge, bright conference room of our new Brickell office.

I gasp and shove her playfully. "You did not."

"Of course we did!" Meredith adds with a soft giggle. "TJ told us weeks ago that he was proposing to you in Alaska."

"Shut up." I look at each of their faces one at a time, studying them. "Really? He did?"

"Of course he did!" Cici laughs. "He sent us pictures of the ring."

"You're kidding..." I lean against the table, laughing and shaking my head slowly as I take this in. "I had no idea."

"You really didn't see it coming?" Aubrey shoots me a *get real* look from across the room as she shuts the glass door and sits down at the table. "Northern Lights and all that?"

I shrug. "I guess I just didn't think about it."

"Our girl is engaged!" Bianca squeals, running up to hug me for the millionth time since I got back to Florida two days ago.

"It doesn't even feel real." I laugh and look down at my hand, the gorgeous, glittery rock sparkling in the sunlight. "I think he spent more on this thing than he did on our new office," I tease.

Bianca snorts. "I know we've been working in this place for six months now, but, dang. I'm still not used to it."

"I know," Cici agrees, grinning widely. "I have to pinch myself when I walk into this building every morning to go to our office. Not someone else's. *Ours*."

"I still can't believe he did that for you." Meredith smiles. "It's amazing."

"He did it for us," I say, holding up a finger. "And speaking of us, let's get to business."

"And then can we start wedding planning later?" Bianca begs, practically giving me puppy dog eyes. "I want to look at colors and venues and flowers and...dresses!"

Cici gasps. "Oh my God. Dresses."

"I see you in lace..." Aubrey studies me. "Elegant but still fun."

"Yes!" Meredith claps her hands. "Sexy, playful, but classic."

"You guys." I hold up my hands, laughing heartily as I attempt to calm them all down, which is pretty hard to do considering the subject matter is pretty much the most exciting thing ever. "We can talk wedding later. I promise."

"Okay. Good." Bianca gives a thumbs up.

We all sit down at the long, sleek conference table, opening up our laptops to have our weekly agenda meeting.

"Okay…" I will myself to focus and not let my mind just perpetually live in the Alaska Proposal Vacation forever. And man, it's hard. "Let's get everything situated for the week."

"I have a new client consult…" Cici narrows her gaze and reads her screen. "On Tuesday. Coconut Grove."

"Good." Bianca points a finger. "I'm out Tuesday afternoon as well, for that big hotel ballroom event we're scheduled to clean after. Oh, do you think—"

"Guys." Aubrey's voice, filled with something that sounds like surprise and some serious excitement. "Guys!" She repeats, her hands flying to her chest.

"What?" I ask eagerly, leaning across the table.

"What is it?"

"Tell us!"

Aubrey takes a deep breath and gathers herself, scanning whatever amazing thing is on her screen one more time before talking, letting the anticipation really build.

"Aubrey!" I exclaim.

"Okay, okay." She looks up, her eyes dancing. "You know how I was going to reach out to Zachary Thorne's real estate agent and manager to see if we can lock down his business as soon as he moves here?"

"Yeah…of course." I nod, remembering the situation. "He was building a house, right? Or renovating it? He should be moving in soon."

"Right. Well, I didn't contact them. Not yet, anyway." Aubrey swallows, smiling widely. "I was going to wait until he was physically here to try and set things up. But…you're never going to believe this."

"What is it?" Bianca demands.

"*He* reached out to *us*! Before I even said a word! Before I even made a single phone call or wrote a single email. He contacted us!"

"Holy crap!" I yell, shocked and amazed by that.

"Are you kidding?" Bianca gasps.

"How does he know us?" Cici asks, laughing with joy.

"I don't know..." Aubrey frowns and scans her computer screen again. "I don't know, but he wants to meet directly with one of the Maid In Miami owners when he moves in in two weeks."

"No way!"

We all cheer and laugh and high five from around the conference table, except for Meredith, who is still and silent and white as a ghost.

"Mer..." Aubrey says, unaware of her strange and obviously uncomfortable demeanor. "You'll be supervising this one."

"What?" Meredith freaks out, shaking her head frantically. "No. No, I said I wanted nothing to do with this account. I can't do that. No—"

"Meredith..." Aubrey levels her gaze. "He specifically requested you. By name."

Silence falls around the table as we all try to comprehend what Aubrey just said.

The last bit of color in Meredith's face is completely drained, and she just stares at the wall, her enormous eyes looking like a deer in the headlights of an eighteen-wheeler.

"Mer..." I say gently, placing my hand on her arm.

"I have to tell you guys something," she says softly, her voice unsteady.

"What is it?" we all ask.

"I...I know Zachary Thorne."

"Yeah..." Bianca chuckles easily. "The entire free world knows Zachary Thorne."

"No." Meredith shakes her head, her expression dead serious. "I know him. Like, personally. We sort of have a...history."

Can Meredith give another chance to the bad boy rock star who broke her heart? Find out in...

Messing With The Bad Boy: Maid In Miami Book 2

The Maid in Miami Series

Messing With The Billionaire
Messing With The Bad Boy
Messing With The Bartender
Messing With The Bodyguard
Messing With The Ballplayer

The Completed Miami Vices Series

The Billionaire's Big Game
The Billionaire's Big Gamble
The Billionaire's Big Temptation
The Billionaire's Big Mistake

The Completed South Florida Riders Series

Wild Ride
Slow Ride
Easy Ride
Thrill Ride

Rough Ride
Sweet Ride
Sleigh Ride

Want to know the day Breezie Bennett releases a new book? Sign up for The Cool Breeze and stay updated on all things Breezie at www.breeziebennett.com.

ABOUT THE AUTHOR

Breezie Bennett has had her fingers on a keyboard since she was a middle schooler writing sports romances about her brother's baseball team. A graduate of the University of Florida, she is fluent in Mandarin Chinese, can dance on pointe, and has been known to shotgun a beer in 5.2 seconds. When not writing romance, you'll find her hiking in the Asheville mountains, where she lives with her boyfriend and beloved Bengal cat, Kobe.

Made in United States
North Haven, CT
12 September 2023

41467548R00136